OF
CO

OF GRAVE CONCERN

OF GRAVE CONCERN

MAX MCCOY

KENSINGTON PUBLISHING CORP.
http://www.kensingtonbooks.com

KENSINGTON BOOKS are published by

Kensington Publishing Corp.
119 West 40th Street
New York, NY 10018

All Kensington titles, imprints, and distributed lines are
available at special quantity discounts for bulk purchases
for sales promotions, premiums, fund-raising, and educational or institutional use. Special book excerpts or cus-
tomized printings can also be created to fit specific
needs. For details, write or phone the office of the Kensington Special Sales Manager: Kensington Publishing
Corp., 119 West 40th Street, New York, NY 10018, Attn:
Special Sales Department, Phone: 1-800-221-2647.

Kensington and the K logo Reg. U.S. Pat. & TM Off.

ISBN-13: 978-0-7582-8193-7
ISBN-10: 0-7582-8193-5
First Kensington Mass Market Printing: July 2013

eISBN-13: 978-0-7582-8194-4
eISBN-10: 0-7582-8194-3
First Kensington Electronic Edition: July 2013

10 9 8 7 6 5 4 3 2 1

Printed in the United States of America

Then away out in the woods I heard that kind of a sound that a ghost makes when it wants to tell about something that's on its mind and can't make itself understood, and so can't rest easy in its grave, and has to go about that way every night grieving.

—Mark Twain, *Huckleberry Finn*

1

I saw the dead girl from the window of the train as we passed the Hundredth Meridian marker, but I didn't say anything.

She was lying atop the bronze tablet, turned on her right side with her knees drawn up, as if asleep. I knew she was dead because her throat had been cut. Her hair was straight and blond and riffled by the breeze, and the ends were stained claret where they had trailed in the blood. Her flower print calico dress was torn to the waist; her corset was popped open, and judging from her bare shoulders, she was young. The hem of her dress was bunched around her scuffed knees, her hose had fallen, and she wore only one lace shoe, her left. Her right arm was outstretched, with the hand clenched, blue fingers squeezed tightly over something.

Few things now surprise me, but I covered

my mouth and uttered a bit of a gasp. Instinctively, my left hand went out to Eddie's cage on the seat beside me, seeking a familiar comfort. Then the train slid by a row of warehouses, cutting off my view of anything but unpainted lumber.

"Dodge City!" the conductor called, walking unsteadily through the coach, one hand on each chair back, as if pulling himself along. "Ten-minute stop for coal and water. Dodge City!"

I avoided his gaze.

There were more than two dozen passengers in the coach, all strangers, and they had been decidedly cool to me. Many were immigrants, rough men and ragged families, mostly German and Welsh, bound for the mining district in the San Juan country in Colorado. But others were businessmen, some with their wives, and the women in fine clothes. They avoided my eyes, but whispered to one another about me and stared when they thought I wasn't looking.

It would prove awkward to chat up any of the cold fish around me and casually ask if they, too, had seen the butchered girl in the calico dress. And I had not exactly been on speaking terms with the spirits in years, so I couldn't ask *them* for help.

In fact, I was beginning to doubt there was anything beyond the grave at all except, forever and eternally, more grave. Imagine all that time we've spent on our knees, feeling guilty, packed in uncomfortable pews, feeling righteous, reading dusty passages in old books, feeling nothing, and singing dreadful hymns of one sort or another. That would be the ultimate joke on all of us now, wouldn't it? And don't tell me the joke's not on you, that you were too smart to believe in any of that humbug anyway. We all say silent prayers when we're sick or we're scared. If you haven't said desperate prayers for yourself, then you've said them for someone you love, at one time or another.

We all do it.

I know I have.

Maybe yours were answered.

But if it was all just humbug, it meant the dead girl wasn't real and that I was . . . well, crazy. Nobody else seemed to see her, and there were plenty of others glancing idly out the windows as the train pulled into the depot. If I made a fuss and there was no poor unfortunate on the longitudinal monument outside, my coach mates were likely to summon the helpful fellows in white from the local lunatic asylum (or whatever their equivalent was here on the prairie).

If there was indeed a dead girl, then there was no need to be in a rush over her. Someone once told me that the dead can wait; it's the living who have to hurry.

But then my mind flashed on the face of the dead girl and her cold blue lips.

Ten minutes was long enough to walk down the tracks a half a block or so and take a look. I had routinely raised the dead in half that time, with hands held and feet tied.

As the train made its final lurch and grumble up to the station, I began to gather my things. Most of the other passengers were doing the same. I was traveling light, but didn't trust to leave anything—especially Eddie—unattended. I retrieved my grip and secured Eddie's traveling cage, and as soon as the car had come to what generally could be regarded as a stop, I exited to the rough-hewn platform.

I was immediately assaulted by a right villainous stench, from a few hundred cattle penned nearby or packed into cars on the opposite track, awaiting passage east. This primary aroma was augmented by a heap of rotting fish, which had been spilled or perhaps dumped trackside, the putrefaction from the flesh clinging to a single bale of buffalo hides on the platform, and the usual mix of horse apples and cow patties ground into the river of mud around the depot. All of this was warmed to aromatic perfection by the sun, which was hideously bright and burning in an unnervingly blue and apparently limitless sky.

"*Fils de salope*," I muttered to Eddie, which means "sonuvabitch."

Pardon my French.

I was brought up in Memphis before the war by my loving Tanté Marie, who grew up in New Orleans and practiced Vodoun and swore like a Creole sailor. I was swearing by the time I could talk, and even though I didn't know then what the words meant, I loved the sound of those strange but powerful words, all authoritatively invoked by my Tanté Marie and mysteriously lacking, as pronounced by her, the letter *R*.

By the time I was old enough to know better, I couldn't stop.

"Putain!"

Imagine the worst single curse word in English and you about have the meaning.

I opened my grip and fumbled for my smoke-colored glasses.

"This is the edge of the world! Be thankful that you are cloaked, Eddie, or you might be inclined to peck out your own eyes."

Now, there's a bit of nonsense for you—just try to imagine a bird pecking out its own eyes.

There were two sets of tracks and the platform and wooden depot were situated like an island between them, with, a bit to the west, a huge round water tank with a well and a windmill to fill it. Our green-and-black-and-brass locomotive was panting beneath the tank, and a long metal funnel had been lowered and water was slewing into the engine's tired boiler.

Behind the locomotive and tender was the string of passenger and freight cars in Santa Fe yellow.

Something moving beneath one of the freight cars caught my eye.

I thought it was an animal at first, a dog perhaps, but then I realized the hunched figure emerging from beneath the railway car was a human being. He unlimbered his frame as he stepped away from the rails, and I was surprised to see that he was well over six feet tall. His derby hat was tilted low over his face, his jaw was covered in beard stubble, and a red silk scarf was knotted at his throat. He wore a jacket that was smudged but not frayed, and over his shoulder a blanket roll was slung by a leather strap.

He glanced up the track and could tell I was watching. He touched a finger to the brim of his derby in a little salute. Then a pair of railway bulls stepped from between the cars about thirty yards down, and my polite tramp slid back beneath the shadows of the boxcar and disappeared. As the bulls approached, I could see the heavy iron coupling pins held in their fat fists, and every so often one or the other would squat to peer beneath the cars, banging the coupling pins against the trucks to make a frightful sound, in hopes of flushing their quarry into the open.

I grimaced at the thought of how much damage one of those iron pins would do when swung against a rib cage or a skull, and hoped the tramp with the red silk scarf had gotten far away.

Like the rolling stock, the Santa Fe depot was rendered in faded yellow as well, with DODGE CITY in bold black letters painted under the eaves on each end. A workman balanced atop a ladder and was retouching the lettering; some jokester had sloppily brushed an *SH* over the *C*, in shockingly red paint. Beneath it, the artist had signed his work: *MiKE McGLuE*.

He had expressed my sentiments exactly.

I held my breath and hoped for the wind to shift while I crossed the platform, glancing as I did so at the low-slung depot, with its bay window facing the tracks, in which a pinched little man with a bald head and a green visor was bent over a telegraph key. He looked more than a bit reptilian, and his bald head serpentined to watch my progress.

"Fous le camps et morte," I told him under my breath.

It's a bad habit. I've embarrassed myself a thousand times, yet still I do it. Someday, perhaps, I will stop. For now, it's enough to say that this was one of my more powerful curses, meaning to "walk off and die"—if you change the word "walk" to that most common of Anglo-Saxon invectives.

I threaded my way through the passengers, trying to hide from the telegraph operator, and at the same time trying to keep Eddie's cage as level and stable as possible. A short run of wooden steps descended from the platform to street level, and at the bottom of the steps was a sleeping wreck of a cowboy.

Oh, about that word "cowboy."

I should explain that in Dodge City they have an arsenal of names for what we outsiders commonly call a "cowboy," and perhaps the most popular of these is "ranger." But for me, that calls up a notion of a Texas lawman, and that's just confusing. So, to make things clear, I'm going to call this group of itinerant workers "cowboys," unless there's some reason to put a finer point on things.

Now, back to the cowboy who had lost his battle the night before with spirits.

He was in full livery, from his spurs to the very large hat beside his head. He favored the color red—he wore a red bib shirt, and there was a red bandana around his neck. Tucked into the leather band of his broad-brimmed hat was the jack of diamonds.

As I passed, one bloodshot eye flickered open.

"Katie?" he asked, holding his hand up to shield the sun.

"Afraid not," I said.

The cowboy grunted his disappointment. Tears sparkled in the corners of his swollen eyes.

"Thought you was a dream."

"'All that we see or seem!'" squawked Eddie from beneath the black cloth, and the cage rocked as he darted from swing to perch, claws skittering.

"Shush," I whispered.

"You have a talking bird?"

The drunk's other eye was open now, and he blinked in hard wonder.

"He does not talk," I said. "He 'quoth.'"

Mindful of the time, I moved on, while the lonesome cowboy pleaded for me to come back—or, at least, pleading loudly for Katie to come back. I heard other travelers grumble as they stepped over him, and a few declared that somebody should summon the law, which made the cowboy laugh and curse.

"You fetch Old Man Bassett or that fat yellow dog of a marshal, Larry Deger," the cowboy challenged. "I'll learn them a Buckeye song or two. Ain't that right, Katie? Katie!"

Now I had a good look at the town, not yet five years old, which the newspapers had proclaimed "the wickedest little city in America," a veritable and rustic Sodom and Gomorrah rolled into one. The city was small indeed, but on this Wednesday morning on the Ninth of May in 1877, it hardly seemed to belong to that biblical class of cities of the plain.

The community itself was a curious arrangement, and it did seem to be two cities bifurcated by the railway tracks. There were two broad Front Streets, one for each side of the tracks, and North Front Street seemed to be the more prosperous and respectable. Stretched before me were a full three blocks of rough-hewn businesses rising from the plain—the Dodge House, which was a hotel, saloons, restaurants, hardware stores, and one establishment that evidently dealt in firearms, judging from the enormous and crudely fashioned wooden rifle mounted on a pole in front. There were scattered homes and a few businesses to the sides and behind. Beyond the town, to the northwest, was a low hill. Near the summit was a lonely cemetery with many wooden markers and a few obviously fresh graves.

South Front Street was largely faced by otherwise empty lots where buffalo remains were piled. There was also a warehouse or two, and, located just yards from the south set of tracks, was a one-room city hall, with nearby jail. Another block south and there were a few commercial buildings, dominated by a hotel that proclaimed itself the Great Western, but nothing that rivaled the enterprise of the north side.

It had been a wet spring, and the dirt street had been churned into mud by the passage of uncounted wheels and hooves. I waded through the muck for a block or so, past the warehouses, and found the odd monument, about where I reckoned it would be.

The base of the low monument was made of limestone, about three feet square, and tilted in such a way as to be easily seen by railway travelers. Carved in the rough yellow stone, on the north and south sides, was HUNDREDTH MERIDIAN, in letters tall enough to be read from the train.

The bronze medallion on top was about the size of a manhole cover and was tinged green by weather. The bronze had the longitude inscribed on it: *100 degrees, 0 minutes, 0 seconds.* Below this was *Welcome to Dodge City, Ford County, Kansas!* Then there was the usual blather that it had been erected by the *Dodge City Committee of Vigilance*—whatever that was—on such-and-such day the year before, surveyed by who's it and what's his name, and it was a wonder they didn't list the hat sizes of all the men involved.

These male forebears were so busy with civic pride and self-promotion that they failed to note the most important thing about the monument: here is where the West begins.

As any schoolgirl can tell you, the Hundredth Meridian bisects the country from the Dakota Territory to Texas; to one side is the moist and populated and civilized East; to the other, the arid and spacious and often bloody West.

But as with many human inventions, the line is an imaginary thing, and only a coincidence of weather and topography makes it such a seemingly perfect boundary. In that regard, it is not unlike our concept of life and what comes after—something that is at once imagined, intangible, and irrevocable.

I sat on the monument, carefully placing Eddie's cage on the ground beside me. I took off my glove and ran my hand over the surface of the bronze, then inspected my fingertips. Mixed with the greenish smudge were a few streaks of rusty brown. It might have been blood, but I thought it was probably just dirt. There was plenty of dirt in this town to go around.

It was a nice little monument, but there was no dead girl.

"Eddie," I whispered. "You have a fool for a mistress."

2

It hadn't taken five minutes to satisfy my curiosity at the monument. By the time I stepped back over the drunken cowboy and mounted the steps to the platform, that snake of a telegraph operator was talking to a man in a bowler hat, who was furiously scribbling in a notebook.

To bolt would have been a mistake.

So I walked with deliberation across the platform toward the train, passing within a yard of the pair. The telegrapher just stared at me agape, but the man with the notebook tipped his bowler. I gave a curt nod in return.

"Miss," he said.

I forced a smile before turning to address him over my shoulder.

"Sir."

Then he trotted up beside me and placed a hand on my grip.

"Here, let me help you with that."

Before I could evade him, he had relieved me of my luggage.

"Pardon, but would it be possible to have a word?"

"I've already given you one," I said. "Now, there's five more. Could I have my bag, please? I am in a hurry to take my seat aboard that train, as a gentleman would have noticed."

"You have plenty of time," the man said, and smiled. He had the self-satisfied smile of a schoolboy who doesn't know his lesson but cares not, because he's the teacher's pet. He was thirty-five or forty, with dark hair and a walrus mustache and soft hands. "The stops here are always twice as long as advertised. The train crew has a fondness for oysters and cold beer at the Alhambra."

"That would throw them off schedule."

"No, because they shave a few minutes or so from every stop west, until they reach Pueblo. Creative, really."

"I don't know if I should believe you," I said. "My grip, please."

I pulled the valise away from him.

"You must allow me."

"I am an independent woman and need no man to escort me or carry my things," I said. "Your attitude offends me nearly as much as the stench from this town. I can't imagine how anyone could stand to live here."

"Oh, the stink is just getting started," the man

said. "The first herds from Texas arrived two days ago. There will be more. By the middle of June, all of this grassland you see around you will be full of beef grazing, a hundred thousand of them, waiting to be packed on cattle cars and shipped east. And we don't mind the smell so much—it smells like money."

"That seems oddly appropriate."

The man smiled, but with tight lips and no mirth in his eyes.

"Come with me."

"What the devil for?"

"Really, you must come with me."

I shook my head in disbelief. "Or what?"

"Face the consequences."

"*C'est le bo'del*," I declared. What a mess. "You force me to summon the law."

"I am the law," he said. "My name is Michael Sutton, and I am the Ford County Attorney. I promise you a fair hearing and an impartial examination. Justice demands nothing less."

I stared at him with eyes wide.

"You mistake me for someone else."

I was attempting to summon indignation.

"I think not," he sniffed. "You are Kate Bender."

I laughed, with genuine surprise.

"You joke," I said.

He reached into his pocket and produced a nickel-plated revolver with a four-inch barrel. I stopped laughing. I dislike guns, especially when they are pointed in my direction.

"I have here a warrant for your arrest on eleven counts of murder, Miss Bender," Sutton said. "Mackie, the telegraph man, told me he thought it was you, on account of your appearance."

"Truly, this is absurd."

With his free hand, he retrieved a yellowed and much-folded sheet of paper and shook it open.

"This is a proclamation issued by Governor Osborn," he said. "It offers a five-hundred-dollar reward for the apprehension and delivery to the sheriff of Labette County of any member of the Bender family."

"Where is Labette County?"

"You know where Labette County is, Miss Bender. You lived there."

He was right. I did know where it was, but only because I read everything I get my hands on, and I remembered newspaper accounts of the Bender horror well. Labette County was three hundred miles due east, above the Indian Nations in southeastern Kansas.

"You think I am she of the murderous family?"

His eyes darted to the paper, then back at me.

"'Kate Bender is about five feet six inches in height, slender and buxom, rather bold in appearance, walks proudly with head held high, and speaks English with only a trace of a German accent. She is twenty-four years of age.'"

"I am somewhat older than that."

"The warrant was issued four years ago."

"I don't speak German."

"You've been speaking *something* foreign," he said.

"Mon Dieu," I said. "That's French for 'my God.'"

The barrel of the revolver drifted.

"Do be careful," I said.

Another glance at the paper.

"'Her eyes are hazel, flashing and alert, and her head is wreathed in auburn hair, which appears coppery in the shadow and flares red-gold in sunlight. She dresses oddly, her preferred color is black, and she may call herself professor and be engaged as a Spiritualist or public medium. Beautiful and devious, she is a master manipulator of men.'"

"You truly think I am one of the Bloody Benders?"

"Remove your spectacles, please."

I took off the smoke-colored glasses.

"I've never seen a more perfect description."

"'Beautiful and devious' aren't descriptions. They're judgments."

"I heard that drover call you 'Katie.'"

"He's drunk. He's calling every woman 'Katie.'"

"What's your name?"

"Does that description include a raven?"

"What's your line of work?"

There was a handful of travelers on the platform. Seeing the gun and overhearing the conversation, they had cleared a neat circle around us. I managed a bright smile for them.

"I am Ophelia Wylde," I said with a flourish. "I am a spirit sensitive on my way to an engagement in Colorado. Let us go somewhere we can talk and reason this out. I promise to be a good and obedient female while we do. Please put that pistol away before you hurt someone."

Sutton shook his head.

"Could you kindly lower the barrel, then?"

He relented.

"Thank you," I said.

"Do you have other effects aboard the train?"

"I travel light," I said.

"Let's go."

"Where?"

"How do you say 'jail' in French?"

"I don't know. I only use it to curse."

"In whatever language, you're headed for a cell."

"Why am I not surprised," I said, and sighed. "The thing that scares men the most about an independent woman is her freedom. It is the first thing they want to take away."

"No more talk. The city jail is just to the south, beyond the tracks. I'll follow you."

"Say, do you know anything about a murdered—"

"Get walking!"

As Sutton urged me through the muddy streets toward the jail, I could hear the conductor calling out, "All aboard!" His announcement was followed by the hissing and chugging of the locomotive as it began to pull, with increasing speed, the line of faded yellow cars to the West.

3

The Dodge City Jail was a two-story enterprise, with the city clerk and police court on the top floor and the lockup below. The jail was made not of stone or brick but of wood, although any prairie wolf would have a hard time blowing this house down. Heavy two-by-sixes were jammed together and held by iron spikes, with the occasional narrow peephole. The walls were thick enough to keep rowdy cowboys inside, and, it occurred to me, to provide a refuge in case of Indian attack. The peepholes were really gun ports.

"What's this?" the jailer asked when Sutton marched me up the stairs to the offices.

"This woman is my prisoner, Tom," Sutton said. "Lend me a cell."

"Lower that piece, would you? You're so nervous you're making *me* twitchy."

The jailer was a youngster, barely twenty, but

obviously unafraid of the older man. He had unruly blond hair, hands and feet that seemed two sizes too big for his body, and a downy beard. Keeping his seat at the desk near the door, he arched his back and scratched the side of his neck in a casual manner. His well-worn boots were propped up on the desk, and I noted specks of red paint on the toes.

"Don't know about that, Mr. Sutton," he said. "Marshal Deger ain't going to like it, you using one of his cells. Shouldn't you be taking her to the county jail? That's your jury-diction."

"Tom, my *jurisdiction* is the entire Ford County," Sutton said, with condescension as thick as phlegm. "I wasn't going to be seen walking a woman at gunpoint across town. It wouldn't appear chivalrous."

"Or brave," Tom the Jailer said dryly.

I smiled.

"Really, Mr. Sutton, holster that piece."

Thankfully, Sutton returned the pistol to his pocket.

"What's the charge?"

Tom had taken the fixings from his shirt pocket and was rolling a cigarette.

"Murder."

"That a fact?" The jailer licked the twisted ends of his creation. Then he drew a match across the rough floor and lit the cigarette. He puffed, then exhaled dramatically while pondering this new bit of information. "She kill anybody I know?"

"I'm not going to try this case for you, Tom," Sutton said. "But I can assure you, she's a cold-blooded killer who has sent more men to the eternal rest than any gunslinger who's ever walked *these* streets."

"She don't look like a killer."

"I certainly have not killed anyone," I said.

The jailer smiled.

"I like the way you talk," Tom said. "Say something else."

"Everyone talks this way back home in Memphis."

"It's like you're singing the words."

"This is a case of mistaken identity," I said. "My name is Ophelia Wylde, and I was en route to Colorado when your Mr. Sutton and his revolver got between me and my train."

"Enough!" Sutton said. "Place her in a jail cell as directed. I will return later with the paperwork necessary to send her to Labette County."

As far as I knew, habeas corpus was still the law of the land, even here at the edge of the world. But I could see there was no use arguing with this Sutton character.

"What are you waiting for?"

The jailer shrugged.

"All righty," he said. "But you'll have to explain it to the marshal."

Rising from the chair, Tom grabbed a ring

of brass keys, which hung from a peg above the desk. Sutton stormed out of the door and I could hear his shoes slapping on the wooden stairs.

"Ma'am, I'm afraid you're in my custody," Tom said.

"I understand."

"Now I have to ask, since I ain't about to search you—on your honor, are you armed with anything besides that birdcage?"

"Only my wit," I said.

"You'll have to leave your things up here."

"Even my bird? Poor Eddie is already in a cage."

"Well . . ."

"The poor thing is scared to death. And he makes an awful racket without me."

Tom relented. He led me down the stairs to the jail, where he unlocked a heavy door of six-by-eights. Then he grasped an iron ring and threw his weight backward. The door swung open on iron hinges, which screeched like a pair of banshees.

The interior was dark and cool. Slanted shafts of sunlight from the peepholes pierced the gloom here and there, revealing patches of dirt floor. There was a bull pen up front, and a row of cells across the back. Tom led me to the cleanest of the cells, unlocked the iron lattice-work door, and held it while I stepped inside.

The cell was about eight by twelve feet. It

had straw on the floor and a bunk, with a rope mattress, against the side. The peephole offered a sliver of the view of the trail leading south out of town.

"Sorry for the accommodations, but we don't get many ladies in here," Tom said. The end of his cigarette glowed in the dark. "A few females, but no ladies. Have you had lunch?"

"I don't have much of an appetite, I'm afraid."

"I'll bring you something anyway," he said. "The lunches are the leftovers from the Dodge House, and they are a cut above."

He walked over to a coal oil lamp that swung from the ceiling over the bull pen. He raised the globe with one hand and reached for his matches with the other.

"It gets mighty dark in here," Tom said. He struck a match and touched it to the wick. "Especially when you're alone."

"Thanks," I said.

"All righty," he said. "If you need anything, just holler real loud."

"Thank you, Tom."

He started to the door.

"Oh, there is one thing. . . . Who is Mike McGlue?"

He grinned.

"You saw the sign on the depot."

"Your handiwork?"

"No, ma'am," he said, and laughed. "Old Mike did that all by himself."

Then he was gone, locking the heavy door behind him.

I sat alone in the cell, listening to the beating of my heart.

4

You have a lot of time to think in jail.

I took Eddie out of his cage and allowed him
to perch on my shoulder. There was no need
for both of us to feel locked up. While I sat on
my bunk and fed Eddie some crusts of bread
from the lunch I did not want, I pondered my
predicament. I was feeling sorry for myself and
not inclined to think rationally about my situation, but it would have been disaster to give in
to melancholy. So I forced myself to admit that
I had been in worse circumstances. I smiled
when I recalled the time I had nearly died of
malaria after wading through a mosquito-
infested swamp in search of the Ghost Orchid,
or when I landed in a nest of copperheads after
falling through the rotted floor of a haunted
cabin in the Ozarks. Nothing bad was immediately going to happen to me, safe in my cell. I
had food and water, and there was Eddie to
keep me company.

What led me here? I asked myself.

What hadn't was the answer.

The murderous work of the Bloody Benders was discovered four years before I was compelled at gunpoint to become a guest of the Dodge City Jail. The Bender saga had bled across the front pages of every newspaper in America. I had devoured every story, because Kate Bender was in a similar line of work to mine, at least up until the time she took up killing as a profession.

The Benders were an ostensible family of four who came to southeastern Kansas to stake a claim on some of the land that was up for grabs after the Osage Indians were removed by the government. On a desolate spot on the Osage Mission Trail, they built a shack and called it the Wayside Inn, offering hot meals and rest to travelers.

Old man Bender was around sixty and didn't speak much, and when he did, it was in guttural German. The old woman was about fifty and pretended not to understand English. Both were unpleasant and feared by their neighbors. The son, John, was considered a simpleton and given to fits of maniacal laughing.

Young Kate, however, was different.

She spoke English perfectly, or almost so, with a trace of what most took to be a German accent. She was smart and charming and attended Sunday school with her feeble-minded brother. Declaring an ability to communicate with the spirits and through them to render magnetic healings, she advertised her services in local newspapers and promised relief from all maladies. She claimed to restore eyesight to the blind and hearing to the deaf. In lectures she promoted free love, denied the power of death, and demonstrated commune with the spirits by some modest humbug—table tilting, raps and taps, magic slates.

Kate also conducted séances at the family's Wayside Inn, where she was particularly popular with the male guests. In addition to meals and lodging, the concern also sold groceries and supplies, which were stored in back. This back third of the cabin was divided from the rest by a canvas hung from a rope, a common enough device on the frontier, and visitors were asked to sit at the table with their backs against the cloth. The backs of their heads made a dimple in the canvas, which provided a handy target.

The Bender men would swing a six-pound hammer into the proffered skulls, it was reported, while Katie would delight in slitting their throats. I don't know how the papers knew this, because there wasn't anybody left talking who actually saw any of the murders. Such a division of labor is a logical guess, I suppose, but maybe it was Katie who bashed them in the head.

Afterward, the bodies were thrown down a trapdoor and they tumbled into a bloody slab in the cellar beneath the shack. Later, they would drag the bodies out back and plant them in the apple orchard.

The motive was money, the newspapers reported.

Some of the travelers carried thousands of dollars in gold, the papers said, intent on staking claims farther west. Others had wagons and fine horses. But whatever a lonely traveler had, it seems the Benders would murder to get it.

You can only engage in this sort of business for so long, however, before somebody comes along asking questions. For the Benders, the end came when Colonel Ed York came looking for his brother, a physician who had left word of his intention to stop at the Bender inn.

Katie Bender smiled and lied, saying they had not seen the good doctor, but that perhaps he had been delayed by an Indian attack or some other calamity. She promised to keep a watch out and even offered to conduct a séance to see what she could learn from the spirits—if only Colonel York would give her some time to communicate privately with the spirits. She urged him to come back the next night, preferably alone.

York declined. Uneasy, but lacking in proof, he moved on.

A few days later, a neighbor found the cabin vacated. Colonel York returned with a posse, finding to their horror the gruesome cellar—but no bodies. Then the good colonel noticed some depressions in the ground in the apple orchard out back, and someone began probing the soft dirt with a ramrod. It wasn't long before the rod brought up a tangled hank of blonde hair.

The first body recovered was that of Dr. Bill York, followed by many other corpses, and some parts of bodies. The Benders had killed at least eleven people, including one little girl accompanying her father. After the father was hammered and carved, the girl was buried alive in the orchard, the papers said.

The Benders, according to a family Bible found in the cabin, along with the six-pound hammer and an eight-day clock, weren't even all named Bender. The "son" was named Gebhardt, and he may have been the husband of Katie, who probably wasn't the daughter of the old man at all. But we'll probably never know for sure, as they disappeared as completely as the ghost of Hamlet's father at the cock crow.

But there were plenty of theories.

Some held the family made their escape by train and horseback through the Indian Nations to Texas. Others claimed to have seen the Benders in Kansas City or Michigan, and one account even had the infamous family making their escape to Mexico in a hot-air balloon.

A few said the Benders were already dead, that a Labette County posse had overtaken them and dispensed some frontier justice.

But, County Attorney Sutton, apparently,

believed he finally had the real Kate Bender in custody. Proving it, however, would be a problem.

There's no way to conclusively prove a person's identity, except through a good photograph or by the living testimony of those who know her.

The authorities had only one picture of Kate Bender, a blurry tintype. It was an image that could represent a thousand young women in any given city. That could work both for and against me. People see what they want to see, and if they are inclined to believe I'm Kate Bender, they'd see me in the tintype. As for the memory of witnesses, it is a malleable thing that can be corrupted by anything from wishful thinking to an outright bribe to a bad night's sleep.

I estimated my chances were good for being dragged to Labette County and forced to stand trial . . . and perhaps even hanged. Juries are composed of men who represent a consensus of public opinion, and public opinion (no matter how those men may think or behave in private) always goes against a woman like me.

5

Women like me.

Exactly what kind of woman is that?

First of all, let me emphatically state that I am not a whore. That rumor has dogged every woman independent of mind or body since Eve plucked the apple. Never have I broken a home—happy or otherwise—although my own heart remains irrevocably shattered. I suppose it fair, however, to allow that I have sometimes used my feminine charm to get by. Violence repels me, so you will find none to suggest I have physically harmed another, and I am certainly no murderer like Katie Bender. But other charges have been leveled against me: I am a liar, a thief, a swindler, a con woman, a free lover, and a hypocrite. Those descriptions you will have to judge for yourself.

I am a Spiritualist, and I come by it honestly.

Spiritualism is a uniquely American invention, equal parts religion and carnival sideshow, a largely benevolent and oddly matriarchal institution that appeals to the adolescent sense of angst and awe in all of us. It has been known now for less than thirty years, ever since two little girls in New York state claimed they could talk to the dead.

The little girls were named Kate (of course!) and Margaret Fox, and they scared themselves and their family silly by saying a spirit calling itself "Mr. Splitfoot" would answer their questions through otherworldly raps, taps, and knocks.

From the very first, the messages spelled murder.

A peddler had been killed years ago and his body hidden in the basement of the family's home, old Splitfoot said. The Fox family dug, but they never found any bones. Seems the basement was prone to flooding, which made the search difficult. But despite the lack of evidence, soon all sorts of people were coming to see Maggie and Katie communicate with the dead peddler. The thing became formalized when the family started calling the demonstrations *séances*—French for "session," but which means far more now.

The sisters became a sensation, and before long they could communicate not only with the spirits of lowly murdered peddlers but also dead dignitaries, including George Washington and randy old Ben Franklin. Eventually the sisters were playing packed opera houses and making more money than their poor blacksmith father ever dreamed.

Spiritualism became the newest rage.

After all, if messages could be sent via Mr. Morse's telegraph, which clicked and clacked, then why couldn't a sort of spiritual telegraph carry messages from the other side, in raps and knocks? What hath God wrought, indeed.

People found this new idea of life after death comforting in a way that the old religions didn't offer. There was no need to consult your preacher for answers or trust that all would be revealed in the fullness of time. Instead, all you had to do was sit at a table in the dark, ask whatever questions were lodged in your heart, and count one rap for "yes" and two raps for "no."

In haunted Memphis, a house was not truly considered a house unless it had a full complement of ghost, and the stories that went with them. Spiritualism was accepted as just another part of the supernatural order.

My earliest brush with the other world came in 1858 when the steamboat *Pennsylvania* met disaster at Ship Island, sixty miles below Memphis. On June 13, her boilers exploded and 250 were killed outright, while dozens more were scalded to death by the steam or burned up in the fire that raced over the ruined hulk. The wounded were rushed by other boats to Memphis, where they were put in the great hall of the

Exchange, and were constantly attended by a battalion of physicians and nurses. The ladies of Memphis also turned out, bringing flowers and candy and whatever else they thought might give some small comfort.

My mother was one of the ladies, and she dragged me with her to the Exchange. I had come to dread anything my mother thought was good for me, especially the Sunday-morning command performances at the Wolf River Baptist Church. I hated the suffocating Sunday clothes, I hated the sermons that preached slavery was ordained by God, and eventually I convinced myself that I hated my mother.

At the Exchange, we passed as quietly as in church among the rows of the men wrapped in cotton gauze soaked in linseed oil. Their breathing was tortured, their fingers and toes curled in pain, every one was cloaked in wicked odors. Many of the victims were deep in the embrace of morphine, silently wrapped in private dreams. Others were shrieking, and some begged for someone, anyone, to put an end to their suffering.

I was not yet eleven years old.

Each of the thirty-two men in the hall was a tragedy of unimaginable heartbreak, but there was one I remember with particular vividness. He was a nineteen-year-old mud clerk on the *Pennsylvania*. As I walked by his bed, a bandaged hand reached out and grasped my arm. He said nothing, but a single bloodshot blue eye blazed from a nest of gauze over his face.

"Hello," I said.

"Annie!"

My mother tried to pull me away, but I resisted.

"No, my name's Ophelia."

"Oh, my poor Annie! Don't you recognize me?" Stoked by unknown fires, the eye flared.

My mother knelt, trying gently at first to remove the young man's hand from my arm, and then with more force.

"Please," she said.

"Tell me, where is Sam?" the boy asked. "Is he on board?"

"I am here," answered a slender man only a few years older than the stricken mud clerk. He wore dark clothes that were well-made but disheveled. Some kind of nautical hat, with a short brim, rested atop a crown of dark curls. A pencil and a brace of cigars were tucked into the breast pocket of his jacket. He drew up a chair and sat where the young man could see his face.

"I only stepped out a moment, my dear Henry," the man said.

The man's voice carried the unvarnished rasp of the frontier side of upriver. It was shot with sadness and—at least I like to think now—carried the promise of wisdom. He was a cub pilot, on his way to earning his license. He had been responsible for securing Henry his position as mud clerk, a sort of unpaid apprenticeship.

"I shan't do it again, little brother, I vow."

The blue eye closed in relief. The hand clutching my arm relaxed and the fingers slipped away. At the moment of release, I felt something electric jump from the young man to me, a kind of blue spark that did not burn.

"Thank you for staying with Henry until I returned," the man told me and my mother in a soft voice. "I have sat here for the last forty-eight hours, and there are some things that are beyond the will of man to control. Many things, to my eternal regret."

"He called me 'Annie.'"

The man smiled.

"Our niece, our pet, the daughter of our sister, Pamela. She is about your age."

"He shocked me."

"I'm sorry, angel. His condition shocks me as well," the man said, tears flowing. "I have humbled myself to the ground and prayed, as never man prayed before, that the great God would strike me to the earth, but spare my brother. If only He would pour out the fullness of His wrath upon my wicked head, but have mercy upon this sinless youth."

My mother put a hand on the man's shoulder.

"God's plan is not for us to know."

"You do not understand," the man said. "I will tell you. I left St. Louis on the *Pennsylvania,* but Mister Brown, the pilot who was killed by the explosion, had quarreled with Henry without cause. *He struck him in the face!* I was wild from that moment and left the boat to steer herself, so intent was I on avenging the insult. But the captain promised to put Brown off as soon as practicable, in New Orleans if he could, but by St. Louis at any rate. There not being room for the both of us on board, I stepped off the *Pennsylvania* five minutes before she left New Orleans, and sent with orders to take another boat to St. Louis. So you see, it was not God's plan that spared me from the inferno of the *Pennsylvania*—it was mine."

"Sir," my mother said, "you must not blame yourself."

"Henry was asleep, was blown up into the sky, then fell back on the hot boilers, and I suppose that rubbish fell on him, for he is injured internally. He got into the water and swam to shore, and got into the flatboat with the other survivors, with nothing on but his wet shirt, and he lay there, burning in the southern sun and freezing with the wind, till the *Kate Frisbee* came along. His wounds were not dressed until he arrived here, fifteen hours after the explosion."

My mother cooed and patted his shoulder.

"But there is more," the man said.

A week ago, while visiting his sister in St. Louis, he had had a strange dream. In it, he looked upon the body of his brother, dead, in a metal coffin, placed between two chairs. A bouquet of white roses rested on his chest, with a single red rose in the center. The dream was so real that he rushed downstairs, expecting to find Henry's body.

"If only I had realized the dream for the prophecy it was!" the cub pilot lamented. He took from his pocket a *carte de visite* photograph of his brother and passed it to my mother. Henry shared his older brother's strong jaw and high forehead, and the eyes had the same sad but mischievous quality. His hair was wild, as if he had just stepped out of his front door into a hurricane. The boy's clothes seemed two sizes too small for him. His outfit featured a vest whose buttons appeared ready to pop, a linen shirt with an irritatingly high collar, and an elaborately knotted silk tie at his throat, as if to keep it all together.

"But may God bless Memphis, the noblest city on the face of the earth," the student pilot said as he returned the photograph to his pocket. "You ladies have done well. Yesterday a beautiful girl of fifteen stooped timidly down by the side of our second mate, a handsome and noble-hearted fellow, and handed him a pretty bouquet. The doomed boy's eyes kindled and swelled with tears. He asked the girl to write her name on a card so that he might remember her by it."

"How touching!" my mother said.

"Would it be asking much if your angel affixed her name to a card for Henry?"

Before my mother could reply, the man took

the pencil from his breast pocket and handed it to me. The pencil stank of cigars. Then he gave me a card.

I wrote my name in a childish hand.

"Ophelia," he read.

"It means help," I said.

"Thank you, Ophelia Welch. You are too young to know what this means."

He placed the card in the hand of his unconscious brother.

The mud clerk died within the hour.

Of course he had the metal coffin, resting across two chairs, and the bouquet of white roses with a single red one at its center.

But I had not seen the last of poor Henry.

Three nights later, his smiling face appeared in the mirror above my dressing table, undamaged as in the little photograph. But instead of being merely a frozen image, this image was alive. His face was illuminated by an unearthly blue light, his features were animated with mirth, and his hair was buffeted by some unseen gale. The ends of the silk tie danced and fluttered like the tail of a kite.

"O-*phel*-ia," he called. "O-*phel*-ia, I see you!"

Then he laughed like a fiend.

I shot out of bed and spent the rest of the night with Tanté Marie, who patted my hair and told me that nothing in the mirror could hurt me. Still, she threw a cloth over the glass the next day. Henry never made any knocks or raps, but he found plenty of ways to show himself when I was alone. His face would appear in a windowpane or on a polished metal surface, or it would form in a bowl of water. Any reflective surface would do.

"O-*phel*-ia!"

Eventually I removed the cloth from my bedroom mirror. "Horrible Hank" had appeared to me so often that his appearance could no longer shock me. Being eleven years old, and steeped in Tanté Marie's stories about magical New Orleans, I assumed that seeing dead people was not all that unusual.

Besides, Hank told jokes.

"Why is a dog like a tree?" he would ask. "Because they both lose their bark when they die."

Another: "Why has a chambermaid more lives than a cat? Because every morning she returns to dust."

And: "What is the undertaker's favorite sport? Boxing."

These were hilarious to my unseasoned sense of humor. As I grew older, the jokes grew somewhat coarse, and I would often catch Hank leering at me from the mirror.

"Stop that," I would say.

But I was never sure if he heard me. If he did, he never gave a sign. Perhaps it was the eternal gale on his side that prevented him from hearing, or perhaps sound didn't pass from our world through the glass, or perhaps he just didn't feel like conversation.

Then, one night while I was sitting at the dresser and trying to draw a comb through my tangle of red hair, Hank appeared over my reflected shoulder. The wind on his side had calmed, his hair was positively neat, and his necktie was hardly flapping at all.

"Show me who you love," he said, "and I'll show you who you are."

6

I must have been asleep, because I didn't know Tom the Jailer, was standing outside my cell door until he spoke.

"Miss Wylde?"

I opened my eyes and saw him there with a newspaper beneath his arm and a cup of coffee in his hand. From the coal oil lamp in the bull pen, half his face was bathed in yellow light.

"Yes, what is it?" I asked, taking Eddie from my shoulder and placing him back in his cage.

"I don't know if you drink coffee, but it is about all that we have here in the jail, except for the bottle of whiskey that the marshal keeps for snakebite upstairs in his desk drawer that nobody is supposed to know about. And he gets popped by more rattlesnakes out here than any other man I know of."

"Coffee," I said. "Bless your rustic soul."

"I also brought you yesterday's paper, for the boredom."

"Only dull people are bored. But thanks."

He passed me the coffee through a little trapdoor in the bars and I passed back my dirty plate and lunch things. I took a drink of the coffee and it was so strong my eyes fluttered in pleasure.

"Too rough for you?"

"Rough? It's perfect."

He smiled.

"Tom," I said, "I have been here some hours and was beginning to wonder . . . well, how am I to attend to personal business?"

A blank stare.

"You know," I said. "Private . . . *business.* The kind the coffee will undoubtedly hasten."

"Oh, sure. There's a thunder bucket in the corner of the cell. All prisoners are supposed to use the bucket. But seeing as how you're a cut above the ordinary inmate, I can escort you to the privy out back."

"For that, I would be grateful. Half an hour?"

He nodded.

"Oh, Tom," I said as he turned to go. "There's another thing I need: a lawyer. I need to clear up this case of mistaken identity as soon as possible, so I think a writ of habeas corpus is in order. You must have seen the lawyers in this town at work in police court. In your opinion, who is the best?"

"Best sober or drunk?"

"Best during their normal state of consciousness."

He thought for a moment.

"Towner gives the best show and is a teetotaler, to boot, but he's more concerned with having people think he's smart than doing right by his clients," he said. "Wilbert is good, but his wife died of the fever last winter and he's been unenthusiastic about work and life ever since. So I'd say Potete is your best bet. It's even money whether he'll come to court drunk or sober, but hope for drunk. He's a mean drunk, but one who swings with words, not his fists. He's brilliant right up until he passes out."

I sighed.

"Potete, then. Send word."

Tom turned to leave, then paused.

"You might want to save that paper."

Now it was my turn to give him a blank stare.

"In case the Montgomery Ward catalog is all used up."

"Of course," I said. "Always good to plan ahead."

He left and I scooted around so my back was against the bars nearest the lamp. I unfolded all four pages of the *Dodge City Times*. It wasn't the *Chicago Tribune* or the *New York World,* but at least it was something to read. There was a hyperbolic article on the front page that talked about how good the grass was this year, and I doubt if any big-city editor had ever waxed more purple:

> Never in the history of the prairies of Western Kansas has a season been more favorable to vegetation than the present. The rainfall has been greater and more regular, and the grass, which came earlier, is much healthier, and a thicker crop than ever was known before now covers the earth.

There was a related story about the first herd from Texas having arrived, a herd of twelve hundred cattle from the Red River, and how the cowboys had some trouble with farmers in Comanche County at the quarantine line. Thousands more longhorns were expected in the days to come.

I jumped over to a story about tramp jitters:

> Dodge City is just now especially favored by the tramp fraternity. It seems to be the jumping-off place for the Westward-bound tramp (they invariably travel toward the setting sun).

Not a very Christian attitude, I mused.

Then I turned the page and found the following:

THE GHOST STILL WALKS!

The ghost of the unidentified murdered girl found last month on the century meridian marker continues to walk with uncanny tread along the Santa Fe right-of-way. Police Judge Frost believes that an investigation will reveal some startling things.

For over a week, supernatural manifestations near the railway depot have aroused the community, and the shacks in the vicinity of the ghostly perambulations have been vacated.

On Friday night, Hoodoo Brown, thinking the story of the ghost was humbug, paid a midnight visit to the monument. He had not waited long, when a low plaintive wail assailed his ears, and almost simultaneously a figure clad in blue gingham materialized on the meridian marker. The ghost was the likeness of the beautiful but unknown girl, down to her long blond hair and the deep slash beneath her chin. At the same time, a light, resembling a calcium ray, shone down on the monument, and the girl rose from her deathly repose and began her nightly walk.

Brown, a good Republican and Union Army veteran, buffalo hunter, and Indian fighter, said that he nearly fainted of fright and has been ill and not eaten well nor slept a whole night since.

Police Judge Frost is considerably wrought-up over the appearance of the astral body. He adheres to the belief that the unknown girl will continue to haunt Dodge City until her killer is brought to justice. He also believes that the poor unknown may have been a victim of kidnap and worse, and that an investigation will reveal startling facts linking her murder to the recent advance of the tramp army into Dodge City.

At least I wasn't crazy. That was good to know, but it led to other troubling questions: Who was she? Who had killed her? And (especially) why had she appeared to *me*? But I had no time for a murdered girl. My plan was to get the hell out of Dodge.

When Tom came back for me, I was finished with the *Times,* at least for reading. I tucked the paper beneath my arm as he unlocked the cell door. By lantern light, he escorted me to the privy behind the jail. The privy was about the size of the average spirit cabinet. When I opened the door, I discovered it was just about as dark inside.

"Can't see a thing in here," I said. "I'm afraid I'll fall in."

He handed me the lantern, and I stepped in and closed the door behind me. I hung the lantern by its bale from a peg on the wall and then sat and waited.

"Tom, can you hear me?"

- "Yes. Why?"

"Then you're too close," I said. "Back away."

While I waited some more, the *Times* across my knees, I inspected the inside of the privy. There was the usual juvenile entertainment scratched into the wood: stick figures engaged in unspeakable acts, a limerick about a girl named Delores, a graffito Uncle Sam.

Then I noticed something bulky down near my left ankle.

I unhooked the lantern and brought it low.

Tucked beneath the bench was an open gallon of red paint, with a brush stuck in it. I picked up the brush. The paint was still fresh enough to drip like molasses back into the can.

7

My Tanté Marie was a firecracker of a woman, not five feet tall and so lean that her hands and wrists seemed like the skeletal fingers from one of the ghost stories she was always telling. She seemed ancient to me, but now I realize she must have been in her thirties. I never saw her in anything but a white cotton blouse, a long blue skirt, an apron around her waist, and a red bandana tied around her head. Beneath her blouse, she wore a necklace that had many strange and wonderful things on it: feathers, beads, bits of polished bone.

My father bought her at a slave auction in New Orleans in 1840 or 1841, when Marie would have been about fourteen years old. My father, it is said, declared that she was the most spirited slave of them all, and a quadroon of exceptional beauty. He paid $630 in gold for her. It was years more before she was broken enough to be a house slave, about the time I was born, my uncle said. I don't know about these things personally because my father died in 1848, the year of my birth, kicked to death by a horse. At least, that was what was assumed—he was found dead in the stable one Sunday morning, with his head stove in and an empty bottle of rum beside him.

In her grief, my mother turned my raising over to Tanté Marie. I never grew close to my mother, who always seemed distant, shrouded in the crinoline trappings of antebellum Memphis society. She did not understand my passion for stories and books, my love of ghost stories and folklore, or the odd conversations I sometimes had with my bedroom mirror. I thought at the time that I hated her. But looking back, I realized she was no better and no worse than any of the other Memphis women of her age and time. It was the lack of otherness that I hated. It was as if I had been dropped into this strange life by accident, that perhaps I had been set adrift in a reed basket on the Mississippi and rode the wake of a packet boat up the Wolf River, that my real family would one day show up, clicking apologies in a strange tongue to claim me.

More than anything, I wanted to belong.

Then, three years after the cub pilot had pressed my name into his dying brother's hand, I met Jonathan Wylde. Seven years older than me, Jonathan was a sensitive and handsome young man with a shock of blond hair, a free thinker who declared that women were the equal of men, that blacks were human beings, and that love survives death.

I loved him from the start.

It was the January before the war, Jonathan was a divinity student at Stewart College, and we met at a stationer's on Beale Street. We were both seeking copies of Susan Warner's *The Wide, Wide World* (which I am now ashamed to admit, but which you can perhaps forgive). I had momentarily slipped the leash of my Tanté Marie, who had become increasingly watchful since I had begun to fill out my dresses. When our hands accidently touched while reaching for the only copy of the Warner book in the store, we both blushed.

We both apologized and insisted the other take it. I agreed, but I suggested that since I was a fast reader, he could call for it in a few days. But neither of us wanted to part, and we lingered near one another, silent.

Then, impulsively: "You have the most beautiful aura I have ever seen."

"What's an aura?" I asked.

"It is a radiant band of color that outlines a person's body," he said. "It's from the Greek, for 'breath' or 'breeze,' and it represents the essence of a person."

"You mean like a halo?"

"No," he said, and smiled. "Only Jesus and the saints have halos, but everyone has an aura, like everyone has a shadow. Your shadow is something that is cast by your body, yes?"

I nodded.

"Your aura is the shadow your soul casts."

"A soul shadow," I said.

"Exactly," Jonathan said. "And they come in all colors and sizes. Angry or passionate people have red auras, great thinkers or leaders have green ones, and melancholics dark brown."

"I've never seen one."

"It takes a bit of practice," he said. "I can teach you how, if you like."

"And what, exactly, do you find so beautiful about mine?"

"It is a remarkable mixture of colors," he said. "Violet and yellow and blue, all swirling in harmony. All the best colors, in my opinion. Inspiration, joy, and love."

Jonathan's visits to the Wolf River Plantation became frequent. He taught me to see auras. His was a beautiful magenta, the signature color of the nonconformist. We practiced table tilting and automatic writing. He brought me books and read me poetry and taught me every secret thing.

When the war came in April, he quit Stewart

College and volunteered to fight for the Yankees with LaDue's Company, an act that scandalized Memphis society. When we secretly wed when I was fourteen years of age, the discovery mortified my family. My mother cried for days, my uncle threatened to bullwhip Jonathan, but my Tanté Marie understood.

"Di moin qui vous laimein, ma di vous quie vous yé," she said.

It was an old Creole proverb: "Show me who you love, and I'll show you who you are."

All I wanted in this world was Jonathan, and I was terrified that he would die—killed in battle, dead by disease, or extinguished in any of the hundred ordinary ways that people depart this earth every day.

Jonathan laughed, saying there was nothing to fear, and he quoted Whitman:

> *What do you think has become of the young*
> *   and old men?*
> *And what do you think has become of the*
> *   women and children?*
> *They are alive and well somewhere,*
> *The smallest sprout shows there is really no*
> *   death.*

He created a secret message, shared only with me. He promised that if he died before me, he would send over a message, proving survival of the spirit—and our eternal love.

Hank began appearing to me less and less after I met Jonathan. The mud clerk's image was as wind-blown as ever, but he began to fade, until at last he was just a shadow in my bedroom mirror. There were no more jokes. By the time Jonathan and I were married, Hank was gone.

While Jonathan marched off with LaDue in the spring of 1861, I waited at home. Life in Memphis changed very little during the first year of the war, and then there was a river battle just above Memphis, and ten thousand people turned out on the bluffs to see it.

There were eight or nine Union gunboats and rams against a similar number of Rebel vessels, former steamboats that had been converted into some notion of fighting ships by mounting light guns on their decks and lining their hulls with cotton. As ridiculous as the "cottonclads" were, some of the Union boats looked even more absurd, like giant turtles spouting smokestacks. Neither side seemed to know what they were doing, and nobody now can agree on exactly what happened, except to say that in the end, all but one cottonclad had been disabled or sunk.

It was 1862, and Memphis had fallen.

Ulysses S. Grant moved his command from Corinth to Memphis, stopped publication of the *Memphis Avalanche*, ordered the arrest of all newspaper correspondents sympathetic to the South, and drove all families of Rebel soldiers and Confederate officials from the city. Jonathan returned to Memphis with LaDue's Company, and we had a tender reunion. Then, in 1863, Vicksburg fell. With nearly the entire river in Yankee hands, Grant turned his attention to the east, and LaDue's Company marched with the army toward Knoxville.

Letters came regularly from Jonathan at first, cheerful notes in which he chatted about his commander, John Grenville LaDue, a rabid abolitionist who had spent some time in Kansas with John Brown before the war. But as the fighting became bloodier as Grant moved his army ever closer toward Richmond during the Overland Campaign, the letters stopped. With every day that passed without word from Jonathan, my heart broke anew.

The war had elevated slaughter to a science, and the list of battles in which the casualties numbered into the tens of thousands is shockingly long. The deadliest battles were Gettysburg, Chickamauga, Chancellorsville . . . and Spottsylvania Courthouse.

At Spottsylvania the fighting raged for a fortnight, including twenty-four hours of the worst hand-to-hand fighting of the war, much of it in trenches. When the hurly-burly was done, thirty thousand lay dead or wounded, sacrificed for a battle in which neither side could claim victory. LaDue's Company was thrown into the worst of it, an abattoir known as the Bloody Angle. Of 105 men in the company, only LaDue and twelve others survived.

Jonathan was not among them.

I was a widow two weeks shy of my sixteenth birthday.

I didn't even know how Jonathan had died. None of those who were lucky enough to be numbered in what came to be called the LaDue Survival Ranks witnessed his death. His body was so ravaged that it could scarcely be recognized as anything human and could only be identified by the book tucked inside his jacket, *Leaves of Grass,* in which my name and his were found penciled in the endpapers.

Jonathan was buried in Spottsylvania County, Virginia. The only thing that was returned to me was the bloodstained book. At first, I felt nothing, and then I believed I was the butt of some cruel joke perpetrated by the universe. Then when the pain hit in full, I wished nothing more than to join Jonathan in death.

By war's end in April 1865, there would be more than half a million dead. Grieving parents, wives and daughters, and sisters and girlfriends, turned to Spiritualists and mediums to give hope that some spark of their loved ones had survived the horror to cross over to a better place. There were even séances in the White House, with Mary Todd Lincoln trying to contact her dead son, eleven-year-old Willie, who had been taken by typhoid fever.

I, too, joined the seekers.

For twelve years, on the anniversary of Jonathan's death—May 13—I had held séances, desperately seeking contact with my true love and transmission of the coded message.

After the first failures, I blamed myself, thinking that my lack of belief was to blame. I strove to become a more devout Spiritualist, and eventually sought out Paschal B. Randolph, a New Orleans trance medium of mixed blood. He taught me many things—including, to my shame, how to use the sexual act to cast spells—but never how to contact Jonathan.

Disenchantment spread like rust.

Like most Spiritualists, I was regularly conducting séances for others. Strange things did happen—raps and knocks that did seem to contain meaning, weirdly knowing messages scrawled when our fingers were lightly touching a planchette, odd lights and sounds in darkened rooms. I would accept love offerings from those who had been comforted with what appeared to be contact with lost loved ones. But when the table tipping or the planchette writing became more difficult, I began to help the spirits along—a little at first, then more later. It wasn't as if I were cheating, I told myself. After all, I'd had plenty of what I thought was evidence that the spirits were real. What harm could there be in giving the bereaved a bit of comfort?

Inevitably, it all became cheating.

As in any profession, there was a sort of fraternity among professional Spiritualists, and information was exchanged on how to give the best séances. One of the first tricks you learned was to visit the local cemeteries in a new city, to choose a few families represented by the best-looking tombstones, and memorize the names and dates. You also would want to visit the demimonde, because whores always had the best gossip. Husbands are compelled, it seems, to confide the most damning of family secrets when in the arms of even the cheapest of Cyprians. Then there were Blue Books for every major city, which was a listing of those families most receptive and (more important) most generous to mediums, along with details about the occupations and personalities of their recently deceased.

Then, if you had a little money, you could order the stage props for a bang-up séance from Sylvestre & Company of Chicago, which produces a privately circulated catalog that offers everything an ambitious medium would need—from self-rapping tables to spirit cabinets, with secret compartments, to fully formed apparitions of cheesecloth, with ghostly rubber faces.

I had their latest catalog in my valise.

We do not, for obvious reasons, mention the names of our clients and their work (they being kept in strict confidence, the same as a physician treats his patients), Sylvestre & Company promised, *but you can trust that our effects are in use by all of the prominent mediums in the entire world. In addition, we can furnish you the explanation and, where necessary, the material for the production of any known public "tests" or "phenomena" not mentioned in this, our latest list. Custom orders and rush service available upon receipt of telegraphic communication from trusted customers.*

I can personally vouch for the effectiveness of their magic slates.

Still, I was not without compassion.

I gave away sessions to those who had little or no means, but were seeking only a little solace, some small sign that their loved ones were happy in Summerland. What harm could there be in providing comfort? For the big money, I targeted those predators who seem particularly in need of a lesson in humility—speculators, politicians, preachers. All men, of course, and therefore easy marks for the humbuggery of free love.

Even though I had become a professional fraud, inside me still burned a foolish hope that my antics were some pale reflection of truth. Perhaps it was possible that love could survive death.

Even though I knew there was no bigger sucker than a grief-stricken spouse, I kept up the earnest and private séances every May 13. I would spend sunrise to sunset in prayerful reflection, asking God to forgive my corruption. Then I would surround myself with innocents and believers in a darkened room and plead for Jonathan to signal from the other side.

Of course, no message ever came through.

I publicly vowed to keep up the séances until the thirteenth anniversary of Jonathan's death, and then declare the experiment failed. Privately, I decided that if by midnight of the thirteenth year nothing had come through, I would no longer believe—in anything.

Now it was May of 1877.

The anniversary of Jonathan's death would fall on the coming Sunday, the thirteenth, four days hence. There would be one last séance— if I could get out of jail. Getting sprung required cash for bail, and I was as broke as the Ten Commandments.

Being acquitted of the charges altogether was even more unlikely.

If nothing else, I would be found guilty by association.

In the last decade, there are two women who have created the popular notion of Spiritualism for the American public. One is Kate Bender. The other is Victoria Woodhull. Both claimed contact with the dead, both advocated free love, and both were widely regarded as prostitutes. One is a murderer and, presumably, a fugitive. The other ran for president on the women's rights ticket and was portrayed by the cartoonist Thomas Nast as the bride of Satan.

A jury of Kansas men would gladly hang me in their stead.

8

As Eddie perched on my shoulder and teased my hair with his beak, I heard keys rattle in the heavy door to the bull pen. Tom the Jailer appeared once more.

He strode into the jail, dragging behind him the polite tramp I had seen earlier. The red silk scarf hung loosely around his neck, the derby was gone, and his coat was ripped beneath the arms. Blood dribbled from his nose and onto his once-white shirt.

"Tom!" I scolded.

"I didn't do it," Tom said. "It was the railway bulldogs, the private dicks. They left him like this over on the south tracks."

"What did he do?"

"You mean in addition to being a vagrant? They wanted his name and his hometown so they could put it in their report. He refused to answer, so they roughed him up."

"And you're jailing him for being assaulted?"

"No, I'm jailing him for his own protection," Tom said. "Otherwise, with the tramp hysteria being what it is, they just might kill him."

The Panic of 1873 came the September after the Bender murders were discovered. Even now, the country still remained on its knees from the collapse of the investment banks on Wall Street. Thousands of men were out of work and hitching rides in, or under, or on top of, boxcars from town to town. But the newspapers chose to ignore the obvious (the papers were owned by wealthy men, after all) and called these unfortunates a great and threatening "tramp army." These were men, the editors said, who had learned to forage and bivouac as soldiers during the Civil War and who now chafed at the bonds of work, home, and family. It was all *merde,* as my Tanté Marie would say.

"Is he badly hurt?"

"He's not too busted up," Tom said, locking the door behind him. "At least as far as I can tell, but he hasn't said a word to me. Stubborn, I guess. I reckon he'll be black-and-blue for a few days, but nothing worse."

The tramp moaned.

"Is there nothing you can do for him?"

"I'll bring him dinner directly," Tom said. "Yours too."

"Is it that late?"

"It's getting along to five," Tom said. "Have you been asleep?"

"In a manner of speaking," I said.

Tom left and I stared at the poor tramp. He was curled on his side, knees drawn to his chest, his face turned to the wall.

The world is unfair, life is pain, but to retreat is a mistake.

"Take heart," I said.

No response.

"Empty words, you're thinking, but I know what you're feeling right now. I have been beaten down, many times, both physically and emotionally, and the trick is to refuse to allow them to convince you that you're worthless. That's what they do best, getting us to defeat ourselves."

He was listening, I could tell, because he had slowed his breathing.

"I'm sorry about what they did to you, but sorry won't help. I don't know what's going to happen to either of us, but I promise that if I can be of some help to you, I will. And I expect the same in return."

More silence.

"Another thing—I suspect that you're not unwilling to talk, you're unable. You're mute, and they did not give you enough time to write your name."

He turned and looked at me.

"Enough talk," I said. "Take your rest."

9

Bartholomew Potete, Esquire, looked like a grizzly bear that somebody had stuffed into Sunday clothes. He was also drunk as Falstaff. When Tom opened the door of the jail for him, the big man could hardly stand. He took a few staggering steps inside, got his bearings, then launched himself toward the row of cells. He grabbed a double handful of bars and then hung there until Tom brought him a stool.

"Thanks, my boy."

No trace of a slur.

"You may go, Tom. I should talk to my client alone."

"Really?" Tom's voice was thick with disappointment. "But what about the tramp?"

"He will be no bother, as he appears to be asleep."

"Oh, all right," Tom said. "I was going to go outside and roll me a Durham's anyway."

He banged the door behind him.

"Miss," Potete said, turning his florid face toward mine. His breath was like a barroom floor, and I put a hand over my nose to keep from choking.

"I apologize for my breath," he said. "I have been celebrating."

"Celebrating what?"

"Wednesday," he said. "Now, they tell me that Counselor Sutton suspects you of being the notorious Kate Bender. Is this true?"

"It's true that he thinks I am."

"While I will concede there are certain superficial characteristics that you share with the description of the infamous murderess of the prairie—you are mysterious and pulchritudinous—that does not mean you should suffer for her crimes. Now, I have an important question to ask."

"Go on."

"Have you any money?"

I was not offended. This was a conversation between professionals.

"Not at the moment," I said. "But I will pay whatever you require."

"How?"

"I have means," I said. "I will send you the money from Colorado."

"I think not," he said. "Payment is due promptly upon services rendered. Is that a bird in a cage there, or am I seeing things?"

I assured him the bird was real.

"I am a Spiritualist and medium," I said. "Arrange my release and I will present in two days the greatest spook show ever convened on Kansas soil. You will share in the profit."

"It sounds like a risky proposition. This town has a poor history of tolerating humbug."

"The risk is mine," I said. "If anyone is to be run out of town on a rail, or dogged by humiliation to the next town, it will be me. You are an officer of the court and safely insulated from accusations of fraud."

"Equal shares?"

"No," I said. "The risk is mine."

"It is difficult to risk anything behind bars," he said.

There was silence between us for perhaps half a minute.

All I wanted to do was leave Dodge City. Why did everyone have to make it difficult?

"All right," I said finally. "But I want the sleeping man released with me."

"The tramp? Why?"

"I need him."

"He's a vagrant," Potete said. "He must be able to demonstrate visible means of support before Judge Frost will allow him to remain in town."

"Then say, truthfully, that the man is now in my employ."

"Very well," Potete said. "We must now go upstairs before Police Judge Frost."

"Frost will hear the writ of habeas corpus?"

"No," Potete said. "That will be for the district court to decide. But Frost is the city's police judge, and he has jurisdiction over this establishment. I will petition him for your release, pending your charges being heard in district court."

"You believe he will release me, just like that? Isn't he afraid that I would make a run for it?"

Potete smiled.

"Miss," he said. "Dodge City is an island of civilization in a vast ocean of grass. I will guarantee your appearance to the court—and inform the depot master that you are not to be allowed to board any train. The stage comes only once a week. Unless you are prepared to walk by yourself into the trackless plain, or tag along with some buffalo hunters or freighters bound for the Indian reserve, I am afraid you are stuck here."

I nodded in resignation.

"Now, is there anything else I should know about you?" Potete asked.

"I come from Chicago," I said. "If—if a man by the name of Armbruster comes looking for me, be wary. Tell him nothing."

"A domestic matter?"

"A serious matter."

"Just what happened in Chicago?"

"It is of no concern to Dodge City."

He smiled, then rubbed the stubble on his chin with the back of his paw.

"If you say so."

Then Potete shouted for Tom the Jailer.

"That's all?" I asked. "Don't you want to know my name?"

Potete rose unsteadily to his feet. He turned his great head and regarded me with blood-shot, ursine eyes.

"Would it matter?" he asked.

10

Upon our release from the city jail, I again took to the muddy streets with Eddie, in his cage, to find lodging on the north side of the tracks. I had just stepped onto Bridge Street, south of the depot, when I encountered an approaching juggernaut of hooves and wheels that made me shudder.

It was a train of freight wagons, pulled by perhaps three dozen oxen with great horns. Each of the tall-sided wagons was bigger than a railway car. The rear wheels were taller than a man, and every wagon was heaped full of untold thousands of buffalo hides. The lead oxen were struggling, mud flying from their churning hooves. Their eyes were wild and their necks strained against the load, while the bullwhackers cursed and whipped the team onward to keep the wagons from becoming hopelessly mired.

The bullwhackers—a colorful frontier name for those men who drive the oxen—were a filthy lot, in clothes made of hides and buckskins, with wild rolling eyes and tangled hair. They loped alongside the oxen, snarling and cracking their fearsome whips, seeming altogether like a pack of animals instead of men. The lead bullwhacker, a tall man with billowing gray hair, was astride the ox nearest the starboard front wheel. He was perhaps fifty years old, with hollow eyes and a hard jaw covered with stubble. Every time he opened his mouth, a stream of profanity issued that would have made Satan blush.

Then a front wheel of the lead wagon fell into a hole and must have found a boulder, because the wheel splintered, the axle turned, and the wagon lurched precariously to the side, driven by the momentum of the tens of thousands of tons behind.

"Brakes, goddamn it!" the lead bullwhacker, the old one with the gray hair, shouted. "Brakes!"

The train came to a shuddering stop, with the lead wagon balanced over the wheel, which was submerged in mud nearly to the axle. Then the great wagon swayed the other way, righting itself with a crash.

"One month and a hundred and eighty goddamn miles from Texas and we drop a wheel two son-of-a-bitching blocks from the hide lot!" the bullwhacker shouted. He jumped off the back of the ox, popped his whip, and kicked mud at the nearest subordinate whacker, who yelped and dashed away.

"You'd better run, you dog!" the master bullwhacker shouted. "I'm leading a crew of *animals*. You don't have the sense God gave a spaniel, and I pay for it every goddamned day."

A man in a black satin shirt, peppered with dust, came riding up on a black horse to the lead wagon and began laughing. He was obviously with the train, perhaps as protection. He carried a big rifle butt-first in a saddle scabbard beside his left knee, and there was a bone-handled skinning knife strapped to his right thigh.

He was a young and handsome man, with long brown hair, piercing brown eyes, and a strip of beard beneath his lower lip. He stopped a few yards from me, leaned forward in the saddle, and gave me a wink.

"Old Shadrach could find a rock in a feather bed," he said.

The buttons on the black shirt were iridescent swirls of color in the sun. Abalone shell or mother-of-pearl, I thought. He was missing the button over his breast pocket. His jeans were tucked into black boots with wicked spurs that had rowels that looked like saw blades.

"My, look at you," he said, in that manner that some men have when they are convinced women are starving for any scrap of attention.

"Here's a girl dressed for a funeral in men's vest and britches and carrying a bird cage. Where in the world did you come from?"

"East," I said. "What is this caravan?"

"Just returned from Fort Elliott on the Canadian," he said. "We supply the garrison and bring back hides. Five years ago, you could shoot all the buffalo you want just a day's ride from town. Now you have to go all the way to the Texas Panhandle."

"And what will you do when they are all killed?"

He shrugged. "Not my business," he said. "I'm into spirits."

He pulled a bottle of whiskey from his saddlebag.

"This is next to worthless here," he said. "You can buy the cheap stuff, the kind that white men won't drink, for fifty cents a bottle. But a hundred miles below the Arkansas, it's priceless. A thirsty Indian will trade everything he owns, including his lodge and his woman, for just one bottle."

"As in the days of Noah," I said.

"What?"

"I'm sorry, I have pressing business."

I walked on.

"No need to be unfriendly!" the man shouted after me.

I put my head down.

Then I collided with something that knocked my breath from me.

It was a figure in a buffalo robe and an old-fashioned beaver top hat, a square man, with dark eyes under heavy brows. Cinching the robe was a wide leather belt, and tucked into the belt was an antique pistol, the kind that reminded me of the dueling pistols my father had.

The creature had stepped out from behind the lead wagon. When we collided with each other, it seemed his hand drove deep beneath my breastbone and clenched something just below my heart. This was silly, of course. You've had the wind knocked out of you and felt the same, I'm sure.

I fell back, struggling for breath, while colors swam before me, pulsating blue and yellow and violet. Then, as darkness smudged the edges of my vision, the sparkling colors seemed to swirl into a tight ball and drop to the ground. I was on the verge of blacking out when I finally gulped a lungful of air in a spasm that shook my body.

"Madam," the strange man said in an accent impossible to place, "forgive my haste. How careless of me. Are you intact?"

He pulled me up with a gloved hand. In the other, he held Eddie's cage, and the raven was making a furious racket beneath the cloth. His fingers felt cold through the glove, and I hastily removed my hand from his. I took the cage from him, brushed mud from my backside, and picked up the valise from the ground.

"Your spectacles are broken, sadly," he said. "But you are unhurt?"

"I'm fine," I stammered. As I removed the glasses, shards of one lens fell to the ground. "Just lost my wind."

"Ah," the strange man said. He removed the glove from his right hand and bent down to pluck a marble from the ground in his pale fingers. He held it up, where it caught the rays of the setting sun, and beneath the mud the marble swirled blue and yellow and violet.

"A prize," he said, again speaking in that accent that was vaguely Old World. He took a leather bag from his belt, opened it, and dropped the marble in with the others, where it grated with the unpleasant sound of glass on glass. "I must have dropped it."

I gave him a tight smile.

"It is a childish habit, but I have become a collector," the strange man said. "The days are many and my diversions few."

As bad as Dodge City smelled, this man smelled worse, like a dead mouse that has been in a wall for three days. I thought I was going to be sick. My vision was narrowed, as if I were looking down the wrong end of a spyglass.

"I am Malleus," he said.

"Charmed," I said weakly.

Who wears a heavy coat and gloves on a warm spring day? I asked myself. *No wonder he smells.*

Also, he was perhaps the ugliest man I had ever seen, with features pale and protean. I tried to soothe Eddie, but he was furious.

"I own this modest freight enterprise," he said. "You must accept money for the broken spectacles and bruises, I implore—"

"'Nevermore!'" screeched Eddie.

"The birds speaks," Malleus observed without inflection.

The whiskey trader in the dusty black shirt rode up.

"Everything okay, boss?"

"Go," Malleus said. "Help Shadrach."

The whiskey trader looked uncertain, seemed about to say something, and then thought better of it. He turned the horse and rode back.

I took a deep breath, trying to clear my head. It was as if a mist had shrouded my mind. My hand still felt cold where the odd man had touched it.

Malleus shoved his hand in his pocket and came out with some tarnished silver dollars.

"No," I said. "The train . . ."

"As you will," Malleus said. "Safe travels."

Then he tipped his hat and grinned, revealing rows of teeth the color of tusk.

11

The Dodge House dominated the southeast corner of North Front Street and Railroad Avenue, just across from the depot and not far from the jail. Not only did it seem to be the biggest concern in town, but it also appeared the neatest, with a broad porch and steps affording the best refuge from the Ganges of mud flowing through town.

"It's not the Palmer House," I told Eddie, "but it will do."

Police Judge Frost had agreed to the terms of my release, as outlined by Potete, pending the hearing in district court. However, Frost did not consent to release the injured tramp to my employ. The city would have its five-dollar fine for vagrancy first, Frost said. I objected, saying that if a man were fined for having no money, the city was compounding the crime. I declared on principle that I would not contribute to such insanity. Of course, my principle was based on not having the five dollars to begin with.

I registered at the Dodge House, but made a fuss about having to inspect the rooms first, so as to think I was doing them a favor by reluctantly staying there. Of course, we'd settle up the bill later.

I chose a corner room, with windows that looked south and west. When I took a glance, my heart sank.

Potete had been right—the grass, which was rippling fiercely in the wind, seemed to roll on forever. Bisecting this field of green was the railroad, which shot like an arrow to the west. Southward, a trail led out of town, crossed a wide toll bridge spanning a creek, then disappeared into a series of low green hills.

I placed Eddie's cage on a table next to the bed, then lifted the cloth. He scrambled about and regarded me with a black seed of an eye that was decidedly critical.

"Don't worry, love," I said. "Another tight spot, I know. But we'll get ourselves out of this one, and then—"

"'Nevermore!'" quoth Eddie.

The sun was red in the west and the town was beginning to stir in anticipation of the night to come. More cowboys were about, and music was drifting from some of the saloons. Already I could hear an argument over a card game had spilled out the front door of the Saratoga Saloon into the muddy street.

A teamster straddled a cowboy and was attempting to cut the other's right ear off with a Bowie knife, but the cowboy was jerking his head so vigorously, the teamster couldn't get a good angle on the fleshy prize.

The teamster was a big man, well over two hundred pounds, and little of it was fat. He wore buckskin and denim, and his long brown hair flowed over his shoulders like water.

"You cheated me out of ten dollars gold and I aim to have my satisfaction!" the teamster bellowed, the knife flashing overhead. "Now hold still, so I don't take more than's fair."

I shrank back and pressed myself flat against the wall of the Saratoga.

"You're crazy, Gary," the cowboy protested, showing far more pluck than his position would suggest. "It's not my fault if your luck is as rotten as your teeth."

Gary held the cowboy's head down with one meaty hand while the cowboy fought and kicked and chewed on the fingers caging his jaw. The teamster drew back the knife—and it was a wicked knife, with a brass guard and a blade that must have been ten inches long—and took a sweeping stab at the cowboy's ear. Just as I thought I was about to see the blade pierce the cowboy's skull, the teamster was jerked explosively backward by somebody who had grabbed a fistful of his long hair.

The blade sliced empty air.

"Drop it," the man holding the hair said, and I thought I could hear a bit of Texas in his voice. He was tall and lean, wore a blue shirt under a black vest, and on his right hip was strapped an absurdly large handgun. He knelt and drove one knee into the small of the teamster's back.

The teamster bellowed in rage. A string of expletives flew from his mouth that threatened to peel the green paint from the bat-winged doors of the Saratoga.

"Is this how you want to finish your hand?" The Texas drawl became more pronounced. "Down in the mud, with me on top of you like you was a steer? Or do you want to get up and walk away from here like a human being? Your choice, Garuth." The man drew out the name, getting almost four syllables out of it.

"Don't call me 'Garuth,'" the teamster roared. "Nobody calls me that!"

"If you don't drop that knife, everybody'll be calling you 'the dearly departed.'"

"You think you're something just because they let you carry your iron north of the dead-line," Garuth said, his eyes narrowed to hateful slits because the man in the blue shirt was pulling the skin of his face toward the back of his head. "If you didn't have that horse pistol strapped to your leg, you wouldn't be so brave."

The man in the blue shirt sighed and nodded for the cowboy to come over.

The cowboy, who had the blood from Garuth's fingers smudged across his lips, edged over and carefully drew the gun from the holster. I don't know guns—I hate guns—so I can't tell you what kind of firearm it was, except to say it was shiny and one of the biggest revolvers I have ever seen.

"All right, Garuth. Now we're even."

"Get off'n me!"

"You're between hay and grass now."

"You can suck eggs, Jack Calder!"

"Drop the knife before somebody gets hurt."

"Just try and make me."

Calder sighed.

"Hit him on the crown of the head with the butt of the gun," he told the cowboy.

"What?" Garuth shrieked.

The cowboy turned the gun around so that he held it by the barrel and began lining up the handle with the back of Garuth's head.

"Do it already."

"I want to do it right," the cowboy said.

Garuth dropped the knife.

"Shucks," the cowboy muttered.

"Thanks," Calder said as he took the gun and returned it to his holster. Then he rubbed the palm of his right hand on his jeans. "Garuth, you have to take a bath every so often. Your hair is full of . . . I don't know, smells like horse apples and axle grease."

"But I just hit town."

"You could take the time to bathe. If you can't afford a hotel, there are plenty of cheap tent baths."

"You going to take me to jail?" Garuth asked.

"No," the man said.

"But—"

"Shush up," the man said. "I don't have all of tomorrow morning to spend testifying to Judge Frost about how Garuth insulted your person."

"But he tried to kill me!"

"You could have lived without your ear."

"But it was my good ear."

He told Gary and the cowboy to take off and plan on spending the night at opposite ends of Front Street, or there would be hell to pay. They sprang away as if magnetically repelled.

Then Calder glanced over and saw me still pressed up against the saloon.

"Are you all right, miss?"

"Just startled," I said, peeling myself off the wood. "But thank you for asking."

"Sorry about that," he said. "They're not wicked boys. Just stupid."

"Well, Mister Calder," I said. "Are you an officer of the law? I don't see a badge. Perhaps you just go about town dispensing justice as sort of a public service?"

"Hardly," he said.

"Are you a Pinkerton, then?" My voice broke only a little.

"No," he said, and coughed. "But I'm a

member of the Vigilance Committee. I also work for the businessmen who put up surety in exchange for bail at the district court here."

"You work for them? How?"

Calder smiled. He was looking down, inspecting my clothing, and I could guess he wasn't thinking anything complimentary. It occurred to me that I'd rather have this man as an ally instead of a foe, considering how decisively he broke up the aural assault.

"I track down those who fail to appear and deliver them to the court."

"You're a bounty hunter."

"Some call me that," he said coldly.

"Do you also collect rewards?"

"At times."

"Then you're a bounty hunter. That's why you can carry a gun on this side of town and the others can't. What did Garuth call it? 'The deadline'?"

"The tracks are the deadline," Calder said. "North of the tracks, you can't carry firearms. South of the tracks, anything goes."

"Dodge City is full of demarcations, isn't it?"

"If you'll pardon me," he said, "I have business. . . ."

"Of course, how rude of me," I said. "Do you have an office?"

"Across from the courthouse," he said. "Frazier and Hunnicutt. I work out of the back."

"Ah, I'll remember."

"Why?" He seemed puzzled and somewhat alarmed.

"I may have to turn myself in," I said. "There's a considerable reward, they say."

He looked at me as if I had just fallen from the sky.

"That was an attempt at humor, Mr. Calder."

"It doesn't strike me as funny."

"It would be, if you knew my situation."

"I'm sure I don't," he said.

"Nor would you like to, apparently," I said.

"I have no time for—"

"For what?" I asked. "What do you take me for?"

"I take you not at all," Calder said. "Your business is your own, miss."

"My name is Ophelia Wylde," I said. "I prefer 'Ophelia' or 'The Reverend Professor Wylde' to 'miss,' if you don't mind."

"Of course," he said, the corners of his lips betraying him. "Reverend."

"From the train, I saw a cemetery at the edge of town. Could you tell me the name of it?"

"You don't know?"

"I would not ask if I did."

"That's Boot Hill."

I left wicked Front Street—and the smugly disapproving Jack Calder—behind.

On Bridge Street, I worked my way north,

then ambled west along Chestnut, where most of the brothels on the north side were concentrated, and then on Walnut. The blocks north of Walnut were where most of the permanent residents of the city lived, and their homes ranged from shacks to limestone cottages, all with clotheslines and vegetable gardens out back. The hill I had seen from the train encroached on the northwest corner of town, with some homes and a few businesses hard against its flanks.

But Boot Hill was really more of a ridge, pointing south, than a hill. I hiked up, discovering it to be composed of a peculiar mixture of clay, sand, and rocks, with patches of buffalo grass and soapweeds. The tops of the scattered soapweeds, a type of yucca, were heavy with their bell-shaped white blossoms. Loose sand and gravel skittered beneath my feet as I climbed, and a few times I slid back a few feet when I attempted too steep an angle.

The hill came to a bulbous point overlooking the town, and it afforded a good view of the Arkansas River, which serpentined across the plain a half mile south. Even at the summit, there was the stench of cows. Herds of several thousand longhorns dotted the valley.

No buffalo.

No Indians.

On the opposite side of town, I could see the brick-and-stone Ford County Courthouse, by far the largest building in town. A few blocks from the courthouse, atop a low ridge, was a white steepled church.

In the center of town, I could see the Dodge House, and it was clear now that it was really several buildings stitched together. On the roof of the main building bristled an array of meteorological instruments for the government weather station. I could see the west window of my corner hotel room, and much of both Front Streets.

The saloons on both sides of the tracks blazed with light, and little knots of cowboys drifted from one to the other. Their rough laughter carried to me on the still air. There were a few soldiers, little groups in blue, having come from Fort Dodge, a frontier outpost five miles to the east.

From up on Boot Hill, it was easy to imagine the cowboys and the soldiers and the townspeople as animals. The good citizens and the soldiers were mostly herd animals, I decided, but the cowboys ran in packs, like wolves. The most unpredictable and therefore most dangerous of the cowboy animals were the loners— the lobos.

I walked over to the cemetery, on the side of the hill facing town.

There were a few dozen graves, identified by white crosses or wood markers, and a few rectangles of sunken earth that had not been marked at all. A cemetery visit is essential research for any medium, because you very quickly gain the names of residents and a brief family history, told in years and ages.

But at Boot Hill, there was scant information to work with.

The town was too new, having been settled only five years before. There hadn't been time for many permanent residents to have been planted here. Most of the wooden markers, at least when the graves had markers, indicated transients, murder victims, or other unfortunates.

Some carried brief, hand-lettered epitaphs:

Jack Reynolds shot dead 1872 by railroad track layer.

Five buffalo hunters, names unknown, frozen dead after blizzard 1873 north of city.

Barney Cullen, railroad employee, dead 1873 saloon shooting spree.

Unknown boy found hanged west of town 1875.

Texas Hill and Ed Williams shot dead for cause, Tom Sherman's barroom 1873, Dodge City Vigilance Committee.

And so forth.

Death by natural causes seemed to be virtually unknown in Dodge City. It would be a healthy place to live if only you could duck the flying lead, avoid knives and ropes, and keep from freezing to death in winter.

The epitaphs were colorful, but hardly useful.

No family groups, no birth dates to determine ages, no relative sizes of monument to indicate status. It was all horribly and rustically democratic.

Near the top of the hill was an open grave, having been prepared sometime in the last day or so, judging from the freshness of the sides of the earth, but it had not yet received an occupant. There was a shovel driven into the mound of earth beside the grave.

Were the city fathers anticipating another wild weekend? Or was the Vigilance Committee just sending a warning?

I sat down next to the open grave.

The sun had nearly set and the sky had turned a deepening blue. The evening star blazed brightly in the west, and overhead a few faint stars were emerging.

I leaned back on my elbows to look up at them.

Then I stretched out full beside the open grave and put my hands beneath my head for a pillow.

There was a gentle breeze from the southwest, chasing away the smell of cattle and replacing it with the scent of rain and grass. It was cool, but not cold. Soon I was asleep, or nearly so.

Then I felt something slither near my elbow.

I shot up like a skyrocket.

A rattlesnake the length of my arm was undulating along next to the open grave, following its pink flicking tongue. A cold thrill passed from the center of my chest to the top of my head as I realized it could have bitten me at any time. I took a few steps back as I caught my breath.

Perhaps the snake was merely seeking warmth.

Then again . . .

"Paschal!"

12

It was silly of me to shout Paschal Randolph's name at Boot Hill. I had hardly spoken his name (which rhymes with rascal) in the two years since he had been found dead in Ohio. The coroner ruled his death self-inflicted, because the gun that had delivered the fatal bullet was found beside him.

He was forty-nine.

I was in Chicago when I heard the news, and it sent me into a deep melancholy. For weeks I wore only black and frequented that city's Graceland Cemetery, walking among the deathly mansions of the rich. I hadn't seen Paschal in seven years. When we separated in 1868, in Jackson Square in New Orleans, during a thunderstorm, I felt there was a hole in my chest, where my heart had been. No, I wasn't in love with Paschal, even though it would have been natural for others to assume so.

When I walked away from Paschal, the rain

plastering my hair to my face and smearing my dress against my thighs, I knew that any chance I ever had of contacting Jonathan was gone. If anybody could have helped me reach him, it was Paschal—magician, mesmerist, trance medium, medical doctor. He was of mixed blood, had been a fervent abolitionist, was a recanted Spiritualist, and remains the smartest person I've ever known. He was also twenty years my senior and married.

After reading all of his books, especially *Human Love and Dealing with the Dead,* I became determined to seek Paschal out. I found him in New Orleans the summer after the war ended, teaching newly emancipated slaves how to read. He took me on as a pupil as well, and shared with me the secrets of his life's misadventure.

All human beings are spiritual beings, Paschal said. As children, having been recently born of spirit, we are in touch with the spirit world. Children are much better at seeing ghosts (and elves and fairies and all manner of otherworldly beings) than adults. But as we grow older, we give ourselves over to the material.

We doubt our gifts.

And even when as adults we glimpse the world beyond—knowing, for example, when a family member is upon death's bed, or being certain a letter from a friend you haven't seen in a long while is about to arrive, or just having the sensation of having somehow lived through an event or conversation before—we are at first mystified, then confused, and finally frustrated.

The frustration sets, Paschal said, because the revelations are all so damned random. It seems that we should be able to control this marvelous gift, that this spiritual telegraph should be able to serve man as reliably as the electro-mechanical kind. Faced with such frustration, Paschal said, we begin to deny and then to doubt our gifts—or our sanity.

But with careful training, some control could be exerted over these other powers. There were a few important rules to remember: Ghosts always have unfinished business, and the dead never lie, although true ghosts will not usually respond to a direct question. If you want information from a ghost, Paschal said, you had to learn to *listen*. Demons will always respond to a direct question, he said, but will only answer truthfully if asked in the name of Jesus Christ or something else holy.

Once spirit communication was established, Paschal said, it was possible to influence the weather, to change the turn of a card . . . and, with special training, to summon the dead. It was a risky business, he said. If not done properly, it could result in the spiritual ruin of the living parties involved.

For Jonathan, it was a risk I was willing to take.

* * *

After three years as Paschal's apprentice, I was finally ready.

We attempted the forty-nine-day magical rite that was required to establish contact with Jonathan. Granted, the rite itself was shocking, but Paschal said such an intense shock was required to break the grip our senses had on illusory reality and to forge a permanent connection with the spirit world. It would work, he said, if our hearts were pure.

The rite failed.

On the dawn of the fiftieth day—April 13, 1874—I found myself shivering on a slab inside one of the plastered and whitewashed tombs in St. Louis Cemetery Number One. In New Orleans, the dead are placed in vaults on top of the ground, to keep them from floating away. I had gone to the cemetery the night before, brushed away the bones of the previous occupants, wrapped myself in winding sheets, and waited for Paschal. By the time he got there, a few hours before dawn, my skin was about as cold as one of the permanent residents of the cemetery.

That's what Paschal wanted.

For the past seven weeks, we had practiced intimacy in increasingly shocking ways: in public, with others, drunk on absinthe, and at midnight in the apse of a church. For the last month, Paschal had allowed me to eat practically nothing. I became pale, cadaverous—and compliant. The final sacrilegious union, he said, on Easter Sunday in the old cemetery, would complete the great rite and summon Jonathan's spirit from the dark beyond.

But in the cold light of that April morning in the old cemetery, there was nothing manifest in the tomb except crumbling plaster and peeling paint. It was raining outside. The lilies Paschal had brought were drooping, but the damned immortelles were as bright as ever. I pulled a sheet stained with sweat and semen around my shoulders, trembling, and watched a water moccasin slither across the wet floor.

I held my head in my hands and thought with shame of Jonathan—and was stricken with terror because I could not remember his face. It was then I knew that I had to get out and leave Paschal behind, no matter how smart or well-meaning he was. While he pleaded with me to stay, I pulled on my dress and fled barefoot in the rain toward the Vieux Carré.

"Ophie!" Paschal called behind me.

I tried to outrun him, but couldn't.

At Chartres Street, he grasped my wrist and spun me around. He was wrapped in a gutta-percha slicker. The hood was down and the rain was streaming down his face, as it was mine, hiding our tears.

"Let me go," I said, somehow finding the strength to pull away from him.

"Ophie," he pleaded. "Stay. We can try again—"

"No!"

"Something was wrong. It should have worked."

"Teach me no more of your evil," I said.

"I'm not evil," Paschal said. "I'm just . . . weak."

"We are done."

"Stay and we can explore other worlds!"

"I have found this world harrowing enough," I said.

"The knowledge of the tree of good and evil is within reach," he whispered. "We can become as the gods."

At this declaration, the square was bathed in a blinding light and there was a crash, as if heaven itself had fallen. A bolt of lightning had shattered one of the ancient oaks and it fell, not thirty yards from us, amid a shower of orange sparks.

"There is your answer."

"Don't you see the power we command?"

"We command nothing," I cried. "Our words are sparrows before the storm. The storm drives us, not the other way around, and all is as it should be. We amuse ourselves with carnal devices and gibberish, as a way to distract us from our boredom or our grief, but in the end the great door of death admits only one at a time, and permanently."

"Ophie, no!"

"*Putain!* Go back to your wife."

13

It was after midnight when I returned to my rooms at the Dodge House, and Front Street was going like a fire in a circus tent. I shut the windows against the noise, apologized soothingly to Eddie for being so late, and barely got my clothes off before falling in bed.

After being frightened by the rattlesnake on Boot Hill, I'd still had much business to do that night. But I had arranged to book the opera house for the next night, managed to place a story in the next day's *Ford County Times* announcing the event, and visited several brothels and made some profitable contacts among the city's demimonde.

Then I went to the Saratoga, one of the better gambling joints on North Front. The place was jumping, and Stetsons were clustered at every table. Faro was the most popular card game, and a lot of cowboys were bucking the tiger and losing. There was also a noisy game of chuck-a-luck, a game in which the dealer mixes three dice by turning them in a cagelike contraption shaped like an hourglass, and near the bar a game of keno was in progress, the white balls being deposited one at a time from the keno goose, an egg-shaped wooden hopper. In the very back was a billiard table or two. I couldn't see the tables, but I knew there was one there because over the heads of the crowd I could see a cluster of raised cues.

I played a few simple rounds of three-card monte at a table that was full of cowpunchers just arrived that afternoon. Being Texans, they were drunk; and in a few minutes, I had enough in coin and greenbacks to pay my polite tramp's vagrancy fine, and then some. I stayed just long enough to charm the Texans into forgetting they had lost money, then slid out the door before the management of the Saratoga could take notice and ask for a house share.

My last stop was at the city jail, where I found young Tom still on duty.

"Don't you ever go home?"

"I live in a tent behind the Rath hide lot, near the mercantile, with six other fellows," he said. "If you had a choice, wouldn't you stay here?"

I gave Tom five dollars to pay to Judge Frost in the morning, along with a dollar for the tramp's breakfast and lunch. Then I asked Tom to deliver a message.

"Please ask our gentleman to see Bartholomew Potete upon his release," I said. "I believe Potete can help him find work."

Tom snorted.

"If Potete has work for him, odds are against it bein' legal."

"Mister Potete has done right by me."

"I didn't say he was a bad lawyer," Tom said. "The tramp has a name, you know. He wrote it down for me." Tom found a slip of paper on the jailer's desk and pushed it over to me. "Timothy Cresswell. He's from Boston. Says he's been mute all his life."

By the time I got back to my rooms at the Dodge House, my head was throbbing from noise and the cigar smoke. I needed sleep, because my hearing in district court was scheduled for eight o'clock. My mind needed to be in good working order, without fog or cobwebs. Yet, I could not force myself to sleep. The harder I tried, the more infuriatingly awake I became.

I sat up in bed and, with something approaching panic, thought of Chicago.

No, I told myself. I would deal with that later. For now, I had to concentrate on freeing myself from the clutches of County Attorney Sutton, paying my debt to Potete, and getting clear of Dodge.

With this thought, my mind became considerably calmer. Outside, Front Street seemed to be winding down as well, because the din had subsided from a circus blaze to a campfire.

Still, it took me another hour to get to sleep.

Then I was awakened by a cry of terror from the street below.

"Lawd A'mighty!" a rough male voice shouted with an Ozark twang. "How wondrous strange. The ghost returns!"

"Speak to it, Homer," another voice urged.

I stumbled out of bed and threw open the window.

The street below was empty, save for two drunken cowboys, arms around one another, staring at a ghostly figure at the edge of the railroad right-of-way.

"Angels and ministers of grace defend us," I whispered.

As I watched, the dead girl began to walk toward the cowboys, her bloodstained blond hair swaying and her dress rippling in the breeze that comes before dawn.

"She's a-comin' this way," Homer, the taller one, said.

"Ask it what it wants," the other said.

"I don't think I will," Homer said.

"You aren't scared, are you?"

"I'm not afeared of anything, Bertrum."

But the cowboys were backing up as they

talked, and were now close to the steps of the Dodge House.

The ghostly girl continued to approach, and now I could see that she had just one shoe. She was walking in a curious lopsided rhythm, as if to some unheard dirge, but her feet never touched the mud. Her entire body glowed with an unearthly bluish light, and I could clearly see her calm expression, as well as the gaping wound beneath her jaw.

"Oh, my Lord," Bertrum muttered.

From a pocket, he produced a hidden gun, one of those little two-shot jobs favored by gamblers and pimps, and he pointed it unsteadily at the apparition.

"Don't be foolish," Homer said. "You can't kill a ghost with a gun."

Bertrum fell to his knees and covered his eyes with his hands.

Homer cleared his throat, stood his ground, and held up his hand.

"I command you . . . in the name of the Father."

The ghost stopped.

"And the Son, and the Holy Ghost, what do you want?"

She stood still for a moment.

Then her mouth moved, as if trying to form words, but no sound came out. Her left hand came up to her throat, as if to gesture that her wound rendered speech impossible.

Then her head tilted back. Her eyes had no

pupils, only whites. And she was staring straight up at the window where I stood.

The breath caught in my throat.

Why has she come looking for me?

"I can't take it!" Bertrum cried, and he shoved the little gun forward and fired both barrels in quick succession.

Pop! POP!

The girl remained, but her blank eyes regarded the cowardly cowboy with a mixture of ghostly pity and disgust. Then a rooster crowed somewhere and the ghost dissolved in a mist that looked like a thousand blue fireflies swirling into the night.

14

The district judge was a man who looked as if he had been turned out by the same machines that made barbed wire. He was a hard man with a hard name, silver hair as coarse as a scrub brush, and his features looked sharp enough to draw blood.

Judge Grout cleared his throat, balanced his spectacles on the bridge of his nose, and looked over the papers spread before him on the bench. After some long minutes, he glanced up, first to Michael Sutton, who was sitting at a desk on the right side of the courtroom, and then to Bartholomew Potete, whose bearlike form was jammed into a chair at the table on the right side of the room, where I sat. Potete smelled like he had spent the night in a barrel of whiskey.

"Mister Sutton," Judge Grout said. He removed the glasses and tapped the paper in front of him. "According to this, you believe this woman before me is the infamous Kate Bender."

Sutton came to his feet, buttoning his jacket over his vest.

"That's correct, Your Honor."

"And you have detained her since yesterday morning?"

"That's when I took her into custody, yes."

"She spent the night in the county jail?"

"If it please, Your Honor," Potete said. He grasped the edge of the table and hauled himself up. "My colleague Michael Sutton delivered my client to the city jail, and to keep her from having to spend the night in proximity to a rangy bunch of Texas cowboys sleeping off a night of fun, Police Judge Frost released her on my promise that she would appear before district court. She passed the night safely at the Dodge House."

"You are drunk, Mister Potete."

"No, Your Honor. I have an ear complaint that has impaired my balance, I'm afraid. I apologize for, ah, any inconvenience my slight list to starboard may cause the court. In front of you also is my writ of habeas corpus."

"You claim the charges are without foundation?"

"They are as lacking in foundation as the privy that was tipped Election Day behind the Long Branch Saloon, and they smell about as bad."

"That will be enough humor, Mister Potete."

"Sorry, Your Honor."

"Who is this woman, then?" the judge asked, reclining back in his leather chair. "And why is she dressed so strangely? Is that the custom now, in the East, for women to dress as men? And is she in mourning?"

"While my client's manner of dress is not in question here, we will be happy to respond to all of the court's questions, provided that County Attorney Sutton provides sufficient evidence for detaining my client."

"Very well," Grout said. "Mister Sutton?"

"Your Honor has a copy of the warrant for the arrest of one Kate Bender, as issued by Governor Thomas Osborn on May 17, 1873," Sutton said. "If you read the description, you will find that it fits this woman like a glove. Also, I heard a familiar address her at the depot as 'Katie'—a name she denied when questioned. In all, she acted in a very suspicious manner, and used all of her cunning in an attempt to get back on the train. Her behavior was so suspicious, in fact, that her detention would have been warranted even without the force of the document. It was obvious that this woman was up to no good."

"So you're saying that we can detain citizens attempting to board public transportation solely on the basis of odd or eccentric behavior?"

"Of course, Your Honor. It is a matter of public safety."

"She *is* strangely dressed," the judge seconded.

"If I may," Potete said. "My client was in a hurry to get back on board the train to resume her trip to Colorado, where she has pressing business."

"Exactly what is your client's business?"

Grout placed his forearms on the bench and leaned forward.

"Religion, Your Honor."

"Go on."

"I fail to see how this is relevant to—" Sutton objected.

"I will determine the relevance," Grout interrupted. "Explain."

Potete closed his eyes and swayed a bit; then his eyes snapped back open.

"Her name is The Reverend Professor Ophelia Wylde and she is a noted Spiritualist and trance medium," Potete said. "In fact, she is making the most of her unexpected stay in Dodge City by performing at the opera house tonight."

"Just what will she perform?"

"An educational program that incorporates a literary survey of spiritual themes, to be followed by modern feats of clairvoyance, magnetic healing, and perhaps communication with the dead."

"But only if the spirits are willing," I said.

"Please," Potete said, placing his sweaty paw on my shoulder, "you are to speak only when addressed."

"No, I'd like to hear what The Reverend Professor Wylde has to say," Grout said. "I recall reading in the papers at the time of the ghastly murders that the monster Kate Bender claimed similar powers."

Potete pulled me to my feet.

"Well?" Grout asked. "Speak up!"

"I do not know what this Bender woman claimed," I said. "All I know is what I myself am able to prove through demonstration—that communication with the spirit world is possible."

"So you are a necromancer?"

"No, Your Honor," I said. "Necromancers talk to the dead for only one purpose, and that is to divine the future for personal gain. I talk to the dead to comfort those who grieve."

Judge Grout ran a hand over his forehead. He had lost someone close to him, and not all that long ago, because I could see the sparkle of tears in the corners of his eyes. He drew a handkerchief from his pocket and mopped his brow—and eyes.

"This is all very irregular," he declared.

"I have to agree, Your Honor. My gift is an unusual one."

"But why is it necessary for you to dress like a man to employ these other powers?"

"It is not at all necessary," I said. "My powers

have nothing to do with the way I dress. The reason I dress like a man is to protest the way women are treated in this country. We cannot vote, serve on a jury, or if we're married, we are required to surrender all of our property to our husbands—"

Grout held up his hand.

"If you'd like to vote, you can move to Wyoming Territory," he said. "For the last eight years up there, they've allowed women to vote, God help them. Here in Kansas, we denied suffrage for both blacks and women once and for all in 1867, and I do not intend to reopen dead arguments."

"I apologize, Your Honor. I am a woman of strong conviction."

"Your sex usually are," Grout said, frowning. "Tell me, why do you look so haggard if you spent the night at the Dodge House?"

"I got little sleep for worry about the hearing this morning."

"There's some wisdom, at last," Grout said.

He took a pocket watch from his vest, popped open the lid, and thoughtfully studied it.

"Time," he said, finally. "Time is the one thing that we cannot navigate or recover. We can restore money to an individual, or even help him regain health through proper treatment. But once spent, time is gone. And if only we could travel back in time, just four years, then it would be an easy matter to settle this question that Mister Sutton, perhaps foolishly, has raised. But what a grave mistake it would be, Miss Wylde, if I let you go and you are indeed a murderess."

"I am not," I said.

"Where are you from, young lady?"

"Chicago."

"Were you traveling with anyone who knows you?"

"Sadly, no."

"Do you have a relative or friend you could telegraph for some proof . . . a photograph accompanied by an affidavit from a friend or relative, perhaps, or a marriage license?"

"My husband is dead," I said. "The war."

The judge nodded sympathetically.

"I grew up in Memphis, but my family has all passed over now," I said. "That is why I am traveling alone. There's no one left, really. The only one I can think of is a business associate of my family, a Mister Sylvestre in Chicago. But I don't know how to reach him."

"Could you try?"

"I will attempt a telegraph, but I cannot guarantee it will be answered."

The judge turned to the county attorney.

"Mister Sutton, what would you have me do?"

"Order her return to Labette County to stand trial."

"This arrest warrant offers a rather sizeable reward for the capture of Kate Bender," the judge said. "Five hundred dollars. That wouldn't be influencing your request, would it?"

"Your Honor," Sutton said, feigning indignation. "I serve justice."

"I'm sure," Grout said dismissively. "How about you, Mister Potete?"

"This innocent widow has been all but kidnapped," Potete said. "She must be released immediately and allowed to continue on her journey west. If she were Kate Bender—or any criminal, for that matter—she had ample opportunity to escape since her release from the city jail yesterday."

The judge snapped shut the pocket watch.

"Here is my ruling," he said. "Mister Sutton, you have four days from today to produce a witness from Labette County who knew Kate Bender personally and can testify as to whether this is or is not the wanted woman. Mister Potete, your client may remain free on her own recognizance during that period, as long as she agrees not to leave town."

"Thank you, Your Honor," Potete said.

"Would that be four business days, Your Honor?" Sutton asked.

"Four days is four days," Grout said. "That means Monday! Nine o'clock!"

Fils de salope, I said to myself. *Sonuvabitch, a weekend in prairie purgatory.*

"Ophelia Wylde," the judge said. "I don't think this will create too great a hardship on you, seeing as how you have already arranged to conduct some business at the opera house tonight. Do behave yourself. I don't want to see you in my court before the weekend is up."

"Understood, Your Honor," I said.

"And Miss Wylde," he added, "out of respect for the court—find a dress."

15

The opera house was so packed when I walked onto the stage that night, they were standing in the aisles. If the piece in the *Times* didn't arouse their curiosity enough to part with eight bits to see me, then the rumor that I might really *be* Kate Bender closed the deal.

Even though I had done the routine many times before, from Baton Rouge to St. Louis to Louisville to Chicago, my stomach still turned to ice water just before I was to go onstage. I paced in the wings, thinking about all the things that could go wrong and what I would do if they did.

"It's time," Potete said.

"Let them wait a few minutes longer," I said.

The hall sounded like feeding time at the Lincoln Park Zoo. Literally. One of the cowboys was screeching like an ape and another was crowing like a rooster, and there was an entire chorus of bird-calls.

"If we make them wait much longer, they'll start tearing the place apart," Potete said. He pulled a pint bottle of amber hooch from his jacket pocket and pulled the cork. He started to take a drink. Then he decided he'd better offer it to me first.

"I don't imbibe before shows," I said.

Potete shrugged.

"Oh, what the hell," I said, and grabbed the bottle. I took three good swallows. My throat didn't start to burn until after the third one. When it did, however, it was like I had swallowed lit kerosene—and I could feel it trickle all the way down to my stomach and start thawing that ice water.

"Good Lord," I said, wiping my mouth with the back of my hand while passing the bottle back. "What is that?"

"Mezcal," he said.

"All right," I said. "I'm ready."

With the curtain still down, I walked out behind it, onto the center of the stage, clasped my hands in front of me, and nodded. The curtain rose slowly, and as it did, the crowd grew quiet, all except for the rooster. Mostly, the audience was made of cowhands, mixed with a handful of soldiers and townsfolk. The only things they saw on the stage, besides myself, were a small desk, upon which a taper in a brass holder and a silver bell had been placed. The footlights were blazing, and I stood there for a full minute, staring out calmly above the heads of the crowd, not focusing on anybody in particular. But I could see Jack Calder leaning against the doorway of the opera house, arms folded, watching.

"Our session," I said, walking over to the table, "will last only as long as this candle burns. To continue the magnetic demonstration beyond that time might fatally tax the health of the medium."

I took a match from my pocket, lit the candle, and rang the bell three times. This was nonsense, but meant to establish a churchlike atmosphere. Then I turned back to the crowd.

"Brothers and sisters," I began.

"Is you a brother or is you a sister?" somebody shouted.

"I am your sister in love," I said.

"The two-dollar kind of love or the ten bucks for all night?" This from somebody else.

"Do you have a sister?" I shot back.

"Well . . . yeah."

"And do you cherish her?"

The cowboy cleared his throat. "Yes," he said weakly.

"I'm sorry. I didn't hear you."

The rooster calls ceased.

"Yes."

"Of course, you do," I said. "Stand up, cowboy. What is your name?"

"Oh, no—"

The man behind him kicked his chair violently.

"The lady asked you to stand up, Red."

"All right," Red hissed, rising.

"Take off your hat," another man said.

Red removed his hat and held it with both hands meekly over his belt buckle.

"What's your name?" I asked pleasantly.

"My friends call me 'Red.'"

"What does your sister call you?"

Even though I could not see the color in his face in the darkened theater, I could feel him blush.

"It's all right, Red. You're among friends. What does your sister call you?"

"My given name is Clarence," he said, amid scattered laughter. "Clarence Hilburn. But when Suzie was learning to talk, she had a hard time saying 'Clarence.' All she could say was 'Arence,' and that stuck."

"Where is she?"

"Back in Illinois," he said.

"And you think fondly of her?"

"Why, I think Suzie is the light of the world," he said. "I haven't seen her in three years, though. I would give just about anything to spend an afternoon with her, she is so fine and good."

"But you feel her love even at this great distance?"

"Yes," he said.

"This is the kind of love that I speak of," I said. "Thank you, Clarence, you may take your seat."

I walked down, center stage, paused, and made a tent of my fingers and pressed them to my chin in thought.

"It is in the spirit of love—this mystical and holy bond that binds brother and sister, parent and child, husband and wife—that we have gathered together here tonight to explore. I cannot guarantee that we will be successful, but I promise to give it my all. Our success depends upon our combined mental and spiritual energies. Keep an open mind. Even a single negative thought could have disastrous consequences. But I have a good feeling about tonight and am optimistic about our chances."

Merde! What a hypocrite I had become.

"Let us continue, then," I said. "And remember—should strange visions appear before you on this stage, do not be afraid. And please refrain from pulling your pistols. Bullets have no effect on ghosts, and I am not yet ready to pass myself into spirit."

"She's talking about you, Bertrum!"

Laughter.

I put a finger to my lips.

"We need silence, please. Thank you."

I took a moment, then cocked my head, as if listening to unseen counsel.

"The envelopes, then," I said. "Slips of paper and pencils were passed amongst you earlier, and you were asked to write a question that you longed for the spirits to answer. Please seal the billets in the envelopes provided, and pass them forward."

A few dozen envelopes were passed forward.

"Could someone collect them?"

An old man in front motioned for the others to pass the envelopes to him. He was about to hand the stack up to me on the stage when Timothy, my polite tramp, appeared a few yards away, waving an envelope. His clothes, including his red scarf, were now clean, but his face was still badly bruised. The old man waited until Timothy handed him his envelope, put it on top of the others, and then handed them all up to me.

I placed the envelopes on the desk.

When I reached over to take an envelope, it seemed to the crowd that I was taking the top one. Actually, I took the one from the bottom—a move similar to that used in cards.

I was about to open the envelope, when there were two sharp raps from the table.

"No?" I asked.

Another rap.

"All right," I said. "The spirits say they can receive the question without opening the envelopes. This is unusual, but we will try it."

I held the envelope high over my head.

"What is . . . No, *when* will . . ."

I dropped the envelope.

"This is just too hard," I said, raising my face

toward the rafters. "Please. No, I understand. All right, I'll try just once."

I clutched the envelope to my breast, closed my eyes, and swallowed hard. Then, in a clear voice, I said, "'Where has my dear mother gone?'"

I opened the envelope and nodded in confirmation.

"Who wrote that? Raise your hand, please."

Timothy timidly placed his hand in the air.

"Sir," I said. "The spirits have a message for you."

He worked his way forward through the crowd, nearly to the edge of the stage. I approached the footlights and knelt, so that I would be at his eye level. I gave him my most beatific smile.

"Brother," I said. "Your dearest mother, Mary Margaret, has been in Summerland these past three years since passing over. She wants you to know that she is safe, that pain is only a memory, and that she attends unseen to your welfare."

Timothy's face positively radiated joy.

"She urges you to live," I said. "Live!"

He nodded, his eyes brimming with tears.

I gave him a wink. He had played his part well.

Then I stood, smoothed my vest, walked back to the table, and took the next envelope. I held it over my heart for a moment, while gazing out at the crowd. I spotted Judge Grout, hunched in a seat toward the back. His chin was cupped in his hand and he was listening as intently as if he were trying a case.

"'When will Martha come back to me?'" I announced.

I opened the envelope and gave a knowing nod.

"Who asks the spirits this?"

No hands went up.

"Come now, someone asked this question."

A man in a shopkeeper's apron far in the back raised a pale hand. I pointed, and all heads swiveled to look at him.

"This is your question, sir?"

He nodded.

"Sir, I hesitate to give you the answer the spirits have imparted. Are you prepared to learn the truth?"

"Yes," he said, almost a whisper.

"Your beloved Martha will return to you only when you quit your drinking," I said. "The choice is yours. That is all the spirits have to say."

The shopkeeper's chin dropped to his chest.

"Oh, this is a fraud!" a cowboy, with a carefully tended chinstrap beard and auburn curls down to his shoulders, declared. He was sitting in the front row, slouched in the chair. His arms were crossed defiantly. "These two must be in on it."

"How could they?" the old man who had collected the envelopes asked. "They were sealed and passed directly from our hands to hers. There was never the possibility of fraud."

"It's a trick," the cowboy said.

"How?" the old man asked.

"I don't know. . . ."

I smiled at the doubting cowboy.

"Believe, brother," I said. "Just believe."

I took the next envelope, and then I frowned.

"Who wants to know if he will regain the use of his right arm?"

A left hand went up in the balcony.

"I'm sorry, the spirits are silent. I advise you to find a doctor you trust, study the Good Book, and put your faith in Jesus Christ."

I took up the next envelope, clasped it to my heart, and stared at Judge Grout. The table rapped sharply, three times. Pause. Then three more urgent raps.

"The spirits are signaling a particularly important question," I said. "They tell me the individual who submits this question wishes to remain anonymous, so I will not ask him to hold up his hand or otherwise identify himself after the spirits have answered the question."

"Then how will we know it's a real question?" It was the doubting cowboy again.

"I guess you won't," I said. "Now, please, I need silence—and faith—in order to commune with the spirits."

I swallowed hard.

"The question . . . ," I said. "Oh, my. The question is from a father who wants to know if he is to blame for the death of his little boy."

I opened the envelope.

"That's all," I said. "There are no names or other information on the slip of paper. But the spirits know."

I stared at Judge Grout.

"The spirits say that this poor man has tortured himself for too long for the death of his son. Too long has this man, a respected and learned man, believed that he failed his precious eight-year-old son, Thomas, who contracted scarlet fever and passed over three winters ago."

"She's talking about Judge Grout," someone whispered.

I shook my head and put a finger to my lips.

"This loving child was buried elsewhere, the spirits tell me. Ohio? Perhaps. Or Illinois? No matter. What is important, the spirits say, is that this loving father should know he was not to blame. It was all part of Providence's plan that this angel of a boy would leave this earth so soon, and that Tommy sends happy greetings from the other side."

I paused.

Judge Grout was slumped in his chair. A cowboy reached out and put a hand beneath his arm to keep him from going all the way to the floor.

"There is one other thing," I said. "Tommy wants his father to know that there is no death—that father and mother and son will all be reunited one joyous day in Summerland."

Tears rolled down the judge's face.

Three cowboys offered bandanas.

Cheers and applause rocked the hall.

Jack Calder walked out.

I went on telepathically reading questions and giving miraculous answers from the other side. The doubting cowboy was right, of course; it was all a trick, an old con known as "the One Ahead." There was no tampering of the questions. Only, Timothy had been my confederate, and the envelope he gave to the old man to pass up contained a slip of paper that said nothing.

With a practiced hand, I had drawn my first envelope from the bottom of the stack, which turned out to be from the shopkeeper about his errant wife. From then on, I was always one question ahead, but appeared to have known the contents of each before they were opened. I had made up the story (and the question) about the dead mother and Potete had instructed Timothy to respond enthusiastically to whatever I had to say. Then, when I opened the envelope to confirm the message, I was really reading the next question, the one about the bad right arm. And so forth, down through the stack of envelopes.

But how did I know that Martha had left the shopkeeper because of his drinking, which had not been hinted at in the question, or the answer to Judge Grout's inquiry about his little boy? Because the working girls at the brothels had shared these bits of gossip. Of course, you didn't get lucky every time, because there were bound to be questions of which you had no inside knowledge. In those cases, you just said something so vague that nobody could disprove it, or you said the spirits declined to answer. But what people remember are the hits, not the misses, and it takes only a few seemingly miraculous answers to win an audience—and build a reputation.

As for the spirit raps at the table, that was the easiest. That afternoon I had found a loose board on the stage, one that rocked and struck the bottom of the table legs when you stepped on it. And it took nearly imperceptible pressure from the toe of my shoe, or sometimes the heel, to produce the knocks, and all that from a good five feet away. Anyway, nobody was looking at my feet when that was happening. They were all looking at the table.

After an hour, I had worked through all of the envelopes.

I asked for some water—which I truly needed by that time—and Potete brought out a pitcher and a glass. Slowly and shakily, I drank down a glass, and then poured another. As I grasped the pitcher, I thought I saw Horrible Hank's face in the water, laughing madly. I poured the water back in, scattering the image.

Then Potete brought out a pedestal and placed a bust of Pallas Athena atop it (in truth, it was just the wooden head of Lady Liberty, a cigar company promotion borrowed from the back bar at the Long Branch Saloon). Then

Potete carried out a straight-backed wooden chair and placed it next to the table.

I thanked him, and he took the glass and the pitcher away.

"Now, if it please the assembly," I said. "I'd like to share something of special literary significance, appropriate to our subject of study tonight."

I sat in the chair, resting my arm on the table, and turned my face to the candle, which had burned more than halfway down. After establishing an appropriate mood of contemplation, I began.

"'Once upon a midnight dreary, while I pondered, weak and weary, over many a quaint and curious volume of forgotten lore,'" I intoned. "'While I nodded, nearly napping, suddenly there came a tapping, as of someone gently rapping, rapping at my chamber door.'"

I somberly recited the next few stanzas of Edgar Allan Poe's masterpiece, then—at the point in the poem where the scholar narrator goes to the window—I rose from the chair and went to stage left, as if to fling open a shutter. It was then, at the point where the "stately raven" makes its appearance, that Potete, waiting in the wings, opened the door of Eddie's cage and the bird shot out over my shoulder, as if materializing from nowhere.

The crowd gasped.

Eddie flew out, far over the audience, pitching first this way and that, and finally circled around and came to lightly rest on the bust atop the pedestal behind me, swiveling his head in birdlike fashion.

"'Ghastly grim and ancient raven wandering from the Nightly shore,'" I said. "'Tell me what thy lordly name is on the Night's Plutonian shore!'"

A pause.

"'Quoth the raven:'"

"'Nevermore!'" croaked Eddie.

Then I went through the last few stanzas of the poem, each ending with the bird's familiar refrain, each time delivered perfectly by Eddie. By the time I got to that final sorrowful "Nevermore," you could hear a card drop.

Then the applause began, and grew, along with whistles—and the rooster call was back, but this time in approval.

"The soul of despair," I said, "as rendered by our greatest poet."

I was lying. I thought Whitman better.

Then I stepped forward and bowed, giving Eddie the sign to fly up and perch on my forearm. From my vest pocket, I took a bit of beef jerky, his favorite, and allowed him to tease it from my hand.

Potete brought out an empty quart-sized tin can and placed it on the stage. It had held peaches that had been served at the Beatty & Kelley Restaurant just a few hours before, but I had painted it royal blue with a yellow moon and many stars.

My ursine lawyer also brought a towel, which I used to mop my face and hair, and then tossed back to him as he left the stage.

"Now," I asked, "who has a token of appreciation for my feathered apprentice? He likes silver dollars best, although half-dollars and dimes will also do. Come now, don't be shy."

I saw somebody wave a coin in the second row.

"Sir! Thank you," I said. "Toss it lightly on the stage."

Even before the half-dollar had hit the stage, Eddie had spotted it. He hopped from my arm, scampered after the coin, all wings and claws, and caught it in his beak. Then he flew over to the can and dropped it in, and the coin jangled satisfactorily.

Now the crowd was up on its feet, pressing forward with money in hand, and Eddie went among them, snatching up coins and the occasional greenback and depositing all of it in the can. For a silver dollar, Eddie would give them back a little golden sheet of paper with a Bible verse printed on it, from 1 Corinthians 12:8–10:

For to one is given by the Spirit the word of wisdom; to another the word of knowledge by the same Spirit; to another the working of miracles; to another prophecy; to another discerning of Spirits; to another divers kinds of tongues; to another the interpretation of tongues.

It was a rush job for the printer and his devil at the *Dodge City Times* to get these made in time for the show. Luckily, I had brought my own Bible with me from the hotel room to check the passage, as none could be found in the newspaper office.

The offering of cash went on for ten minutes or so, and the rough men smiled like school-boys as the clever raven took the money from their hands and deposited it noisily in the peaches can.

Finally I walked Eddie over to the wings and returned him to his cage.

Then I returned to the stage and struck a thoughtful pose, my arms crossed and my head high.

"I am a Spiritualist, my friends," I said. "No matter what you may have read in the newspa-pers about Spiritualism or mediums, I appeal for you to decide for yourself. Does the soul survive death? I submit that we have had proof here tonight."

I pursed my lips.

"Spiritualism has three principles: the sur-vival of the spirit after death, the ongoing con-cern of the deceased for the living, and the ability of those spirits to communicate with the living through a medium. But we also em-brace the teachings of Christ and seek the light wherever we may find it."

Approving nods and scattered "amens."

"But the candle grows short," I said. "Our

time here is almost spent. In the few minutes we have left, I will endeavor to answer whatever final questions you may have."

"Can you ask the spirits to tell us what numbers are going to fall from the keno goose tomorrow night at the Sarasota?"

Laughter.

"I'm sorry," I said. "Spirit communication aimed at foretelling the future for personal gain is forbidden by the Book."

An uncomfortable silence followed.

"But surely you have other questions," I suggested. "In the past, I have established spirit communication with figures such as Benjamin Franklin, Thomas Jefferson, and even George Washington. Is there nothing you would ask of these sages?"

A soldier of perhaps twenty put his hand in the air.

"Yes, Corporal."

"Can you talk to General Custer?"

George Armstrong Custer and more than two hundred men in his command had died in June the year before at the Battle of the Little Bighorn in Montana Territory. His death had become a national obsession and had renewed fear of Indian attacks across the West.

"I don't know," I said. "What would you like to ask him?"

"What it was like—you know—at the end? Nobody knows what happened."

Nobody but a couple thousand Indians, I thought.

"All right, then," I said. "Let us try."

I put my palms down, motioning for silence; then I crossed my arms. I closed my eyes and threw my head back. My head tilted from side to side as my eyelids fluttered. I had to decide what voice to use.

Typically, a trance medium will pretend to speak through a spirit guide. For Victoria Woodhull, it was the ancient Greek orator Demosthenes. For many lesser mediums—including me—it had often been a Native American spirit, and mine was an Indian princess, Prairie Flower. This played well east of the Mississippi; but in the West, there was still such a fear of Indian attack that I thought better of using the Native American voice. Also, it seemed ludicrous for an Indian princess—or any Indian—to interrogate Custer.

So I decided just to be myself.

"George Armstrong Custer," I said. "Are you there, General Custer?"

A pause.

"General Custer! It is The Reverend Professor Ophelia Wylde."

Another long pause.

"Yes! Go on."

I struck a pose of listening intently.

"General, I understand. Safe travels."

I opened my eyes.

"I'm sorry, Corporal," I said. "It has been less

than a year since the general heroically crossed over. His spirit is not yet ready to communicate with the living. But he bids that you ask again in a year's time."

The corporal nodded his thanks.

"Anyone else?"

The cowboy with the tidy beard and auburn curls raised his hand.

"Yes?"

"Are you Kate Bender?"

The candle guttered and died.

"I'm sorry," I said. "Our time is spent."

16

The take from the opera house, after expenses, was a little over one hundred dollars. Even after the split with Potete, I had more than fifty dollars in cash money. It wasn't the best I'd ever done, but it was not bad. Most laborers worked a full month for a single twenty-dollar gold piece.

But it wasn't enough. I wasn't most people, and I didn't work for laborer's wages. I needed enough money to get Eddie and me to Colorado, and to see us through for a few months in a fashion that wouldn't prove too distasteful.

Before I saw the dead girl from the train, and was then kidnapped by Sutton, my plan had been to go by rail as far as Pueblo. Then I could either amble north to Denver, where there were friends and a reliable Blue Book to consult, or I could keep going west. I'd heard that San Francisco was wide open.

There are precious few choices for a woman on her own, and I didn't want to end up hustling drinks in the saloons or washing clothes behind the Dodge House or occupying a crib along South Front. I still carried the horror of those few weeks of poverty after I'd left Paschal in New Orleans, and they were weeks I did not want to relive.

Now, I don't want to give the impression that the performance wasn't work. By the time I left the stage, I was exhausted, dripping with sweat, and in a kind of mental fog. I had taken another pull from Potete's bottle of mezcal. Then I had taken Eddie directly back to our rooms at the Dodge House, where I fell into bed, still wearing half my clothes.

I emerged from the Dodge House about noon on Friday, ate a meal of chipped beef at Beatty & Kelley's, finding only a little sand in it, and then made my way down to the Saratoga Saloon.

The Saratoga was owned by William Harris and Chalkley Beeson. Since Beeson was a member of the city council, I thought it was as good a place as any to rent a table. Beeson was a large man with good features and large eyes, which had sleepy lids. When you were talking to him, it seemed as if he were about to fall asleep, but he heard every word. After a short meeting, in which I did most of the talking, Beeson agreed to me keeping a table in the back, near the billiard tables, for ten dollars a day, as long as I kept my visitors drinking. I needed a public place to meet clients and schedule readings.

Just days before, I would never have dreamed of doing the low con on average folks to get by. Bankers? Sure. Senators? Bingo. Millionaires? Of any stripe. I saw it as a kind of public service—revenge for all of the ordinary people they'd stepped on or stepped over to grab power and money. In Chicago, the target had been pompous Potter Palmer, owner of the Palmer House.

The first Palmer House had burned during the Great Chicago Fire in 1871, just thirteen days after its completion. However, before the fire reached the hotel, its architect carried the blueprints to the hotel basement, dug a pit, and covered them with two feet of sand and damp clay. Old Potter Palmer secured a $1.7 million loan on his signature—the largest private loan in history—to rebuild the hotel, using new clay tile building techniques, just across the street. Potter claimed it was the first "fireproof" hotel in history. He even challenged guests to start a fire in their hotel rooms to see if it would spread to other rooms; the catch was that if the fire failed to spread, the guest had to pay for the night— and the damages. Nobody had ever tried, but even if they had succeeded, old Potter could afford it. He owned more than a mile of State Street, both sides, and was one of the wealthiest men in the country. And he was a gambler, loving to bet on the horses. I've never met a hobby gambler who wasn't a superstitious fool.

How could I resist such a challenge?

By and by, I left Cincinnati, where I had become bored after teasing a few thousand dollars out of a pork baron, who was foolishly obsessed with the spirit of Cleopatra. I had moved to Chicago, and my new address was the Palmer House. It was an easy matter to buy an introduction to Chicago society.

Potter Palmer had just turned fifty when I met him, a grandfatherly man with a crop of white hair. He was married to a woman half his age. Bertha, the wife, was a blond beauty. He had given her the first hotel as a wedding present (some wedding—I'd like to have seen the cake). She had given him a couple of kids, so there was no family tragedy to exploit. But the way I saw it, he was just as married to that hotel, and the specter of fire must haunt him still.

So I told him upon our second "chance" meeting that I had a curious message for him. During a séance for friends in my room at the Palmer, an unfamiliar spirit voice had begged for attention, I said. The spirit kept repeating a series of numbers that meant nothing to me— twenty-four, eighteen, two—but promised it would mean something to Potter Palmer.

He said it meant nothing to him as well. What else did the spirit say?

Nothing, I said. That was all.

I heard nothing for three days. Then I received an expected note from Potter Palmer. The message meant Jeremiah, the twenty-fourth book of the Old Testament, Chapter 18, Verse 2: *Arise, and go down to the potter's house, and there I will cause thee to hear my words.*

Would it be possible for him to attend a séance in my room?

And so I hosted a session for old Potter and his wife, Bertha, and began to spin the tale of Constance Cleary, an unfortunate who had burned to death in the first hotel. He protested that was impossible, as none of the three hundred who perished in the Great Chicago Fire of 1871 died in the Palmer House.

Ah, I said, that was what distressed the poor spirit so. No living soul knew her fate. Constance Cleary was a young and pregnant Irishwoman—just twenty-eight, the same age as his wife and me!—who had been at work as a charwoman some blocks down from the hotel the night of the fire. She had heard the alarm too late. The blaze had chased her from block to block; until finally, a few minutes after midnight, unable to run another step, she sought refuge in the fortress-like Palmer House.

And there she perished. . . . Her body and that of her unborn child were incinerated by the fire.

Potter Palmer had to know more, of course. Where was her family now? Had she other children? Had the husband remarried?

He offered to pay for more sessions, but I would not hear of it. We were, after all, both interested in doing good. Of course, the spirit required certain things for communication. Constance was worried about me, for one, and asked that I be relocated to a comfortable cottage away from the city, where I could get proper rest.

As time passed, the séances had to become more elaborate to keep up old Potter's interest. A spirit cabinet was installed in a corner of my cottage, from which came floating trumpets and ghostly hands and mystical messages written on slates.

More details of Constance's demise emerged: taps from which no water came because the city waterworks had failed, towels stuffed under the door to keep out the smoke, hideous fingers of flame that raced across the walls and ceiling in the final desperate minutes.

Finally there appeared from the spirit cabinet a luminous full-form apparition of Constance, complete with ghost child, courtesy of my friends at Sylvestre & Company. The ghost cried piteously. Old Potter was beside himself. He even climbed inside the cabinet to comfort her. What could he possibly do to ease the spirit's suffering? he asked.

A hundred thousand dollars to establish a

home for fire orphans, Constance said. The money could be deposited with Ophelia Wylde, who would wisely administer the fund using her other powers.

And it nearly worked, too.

But the morning I was to receive the money, the Pinkertons came knocking on my cottage door. Perhaps I had become too friendly with old Potter inside the spirit cabinet and jealous Bertha Palmer had called the detectives to check me out. The agency already had a dossier on my activities in Cincinnati, where the pork baron had sworn a warrant out for my arrest and topped it off with a thousand-dollar reward. It seems he had no sense of humor—or of history. Had anybody who had ever fallen in love with Cleopatra lived happily ever after?

I barely had time to grab my valise and Eddie's cage as I fled out the back.

17

The cowboy with the jack of diamonds tucked into his hatband slunk into the Saratoga at about three o'clock on Friday afternoon. He was still in the red bib shirt and the red bandana that I had seen when I stepped over him at the railway platform, but he must have bathed and had his clothes washed since, because he nearly looked presentable. Also, he was only somewhat drunk.

He spotted my table when he came in off the street, but it took him time to work his way back. First he passed out a handful of cigars, which, he said, were courtesy of Mike McGlue. Then he paused long enough at the bar to knock back a couple of shots before circumambulating on to my table.

"Want a cigar?" he asked.

"Why not?"

The cigar smelled expensive. The band said, *Key West.* I put it into my inside pocket for later.

"I was at the opera house the other night. Remember me?"

"How could I forget?"

"I forget some things," he confessed, throwing himself into a chair.

"Do you think it might be your consumption of alcohol?"

"I drink to forget. It works, for a spell."

"I first met you at the bottom of the steps at the railway depot," I said. "You don't remember that?"

He shook his head.

"Why do this to yourself?"

"Because I am deranged by melancholy."

He took a ragged newspaper clipping from his pocket and pushed it across the table. It was a wire story from the *Kansas City Times,* five months old, about the Ashtabula Horror. A Lake Shore and Michigan Southern Railway express was crossing the snow-laden Ashtabula River Bridge in Ohio when the iron trusses failed and plunged a locomotive and eleven cars down seventy feet to the frozen river below. The wooden cars piled on top of each other and became a funeral pyre ignited by kerosene heating stoves and lamps. Ninety-two people died, some of them burned beyond recognition; another sixty-four persons were badly injured.

"What am I looking for?"

"There," the cowboy said, jabbing his finger at a name among the list of the dead. "That's my sister, Kathryn Murdock. She was only twenty-three. They had to identify her by a favorite necklace she wore."

The cowboy dropped his face to his forearms, sobbing. "Oh, how she must have suffered!"

"And you've been grieving these five months."

"I have been drunk these five months," he said. "I learned of the horror when I was in Kansas City and have been drifting since, drifting from ranch to range, from city to town. My folks in Ohio don't even know where I'm at. Been in Dodge for the last couple of weeks."

"And they haven't locked you up as a vagrant?"

"They won't, as long as I have drinking money."

I sighed. "What's your name?"

"Jim Murdock," he said. "Folks call me 'Diamond Jim.'"

"What is it you want to do, Jim?"

"I seen you talk to the dead at the opera house. I reckoned you could talk to Kate for me." Now his voice grew to a whisper. "There are some things that I wanted to tell her that I didn't have a chance. I would give anything to talk to her one last time."

Just about every ordinary person who has ever wanted me to contact the dearly departed for them has had a similar wish. We humans, sadly, are an arrogant lot and believe that we have all the time in the world to say the important things. Maybe we just can't face the truth that any of us can be extinguished in the blink of an eye.

"Jim, it's not as simple as it looked the other night."

"I've got money," he said, digging into his pocket. He dropped a handful of coins on the table. Silver dollars, mostly, but a twenty-dollar gold piece wheeled unsteadily toward the edge.

I caught the double eagle before it rolled off.

"All right, Jim," I said, closing my hand around the gold coin. "But if I help you contact your sister, you have to promise me something."

"Anything."

"That you'll wire your people in Ohio, straightaway."

"But they'll want me to come home."

"You don't have to go home," I said. "But you can't keep them in the dark, wondering if they've lost another child. You must have driven them crazy with worry."

"But I'm a ranger," he said. "A rounder. A lone wolf from—"

"You're a kid from Ohio who is on his way to drinking himself to death."

"Sometimes I don't remember the things I do when I'm drunk," he said. "I get my dander up pretty damned quick, as Marshal Deger and

Old Man Bassett can tell you. Sometimes I do things I'm not proud of."

"Look, Jim," I said. "Do we have a deal?"

He nodded.

"Here's how it works," I said. "Go find a piece of paper and a pencil and write down everything it is that you want to tell your sister, just like you were writing her a letter. Take some time, because you want to make sure that you get it all down, because we might only have one chance to make contact with her."

He looked puzzled.

"But at the opera house, you said you couldn't contact General Custer because he had been dead for less than a year. How is this going to work for Katie, considering she's only been gone a few months?"

"Oh, that," I said. "I made that up so I wouldn't embarrass that young soldier in front of everybody. Truth is, the general didn't want to talk to a corporal."

"Ah," Jim said.

"Come back here with your paper, along about dark, and we'll see in what shape the ether is in. If things look good, we'll arrange a session—a séance."

"Is that double eagle going to cover it?"

"Let me have the silver and paper money, too," I said.

Diamond Jim looked shocked.

"I don't want you getting skunked before you

write that letter," I said, picking his money up off the table as he emptied his pockets. "Come back at dark, like I said."

As Jim Murdock was walking out of the Saratoga, the bounty hunter Jack Calder was coming in. He declined a cigar and gave Diamond Jim a short lecture about the sanctity of private property.

"Professor," Calder said as he approached the table. He was wearing another blue shirt under the black vest. The shirt matched his eyes. Unlike the other men in Dodge, I had never seen him wear a hat.

"Do you mind?"

"Not at all," I said, as cool as I could manage. The memory of his rudeness at our first meeting still stung, and I loathed myself for it. "What can I do for the firm of Frazier and Hunnicutt?"

"Not sure," he said. "I feel a little foolish."

Secretly, I was pleased.

"Don't," I said. "Tell me what's on your mind."

"Saw your act last night," he said. "I feel foolish because you had me believing for a spell. You were right entertaining, I have to admit. But let's face it, nobody can talk to the dead."

I smiled. "Do you go to church, Mister Calder?"

"Not regular."

"But you have."

"When I was a boy," he said. "Methodist. Bell County, Texas."

"But not now."

"I've been to a wedding or two at the Union Church, up on Gospel Ridge," he said. As he spoke, he seldom looked directly at me. He seemed, instead, to be looking at a spot just over my left shoulder. "But we don't have a steady preacher. Sometimes the congregations up in Emporia or Topeka will send somebody down the railroad track our way, to wave the Good Book at us for a Sunday or two. What's your point?"

"That you sometimes go to church, and presumably you pray to something you can't see or touch. Now, how is that different than what I do? You can't prove any more than I can that what you're talking to when you pray is really there. Just maybe I'm talking to the real thing, too."

"Horse apples."

"All right," I said. "Let's assume for a moment that I am, as you say, full of horse apples. How does it do any more harm than gathering in that church up on Gospel Ridge and saying some words over a body you're about to plant in the ground? It doesn't do any more harm, I say, and might even do some good."

"What you have is a business, not a religion."

"Compared to the other establishments in this town, I'd say I'm performing a civic duty," I said. "I don't encourage the drinking of alcohol, and nobody is losing a season's wages at the faro table. When people leave my show, they're happy."

"I didn't say I wanted to close you down."

"Not yet," I said. "In my experience, that usually comes just before somebody like you asks for protection money. What do you want, ten percent? Twenty?"

"I don't do that."

"Then what do you want?"

"To tell you I'll be watching," he said. "Ever since we met, I've had this queer feeling in my gut, like I ate something bad. You dress strange and you talk funny, and everybody in town knows about your pet raven and your conversations with the dead. If I thought you believe in this stuff, then I might feel a little easier. But I can tell you, Miss Wylde, that in my line of work, I meet a lot of liars. Hands down, you are the best."

"I'm sorry you feel that way," I said, and meant it. "I wish I could convince you otherwise. What would it take?"

He rubbed his jaw. "Do you know about this dead girl they found on the Hundredth Meridian marker? Throat cut, nobody knows her name, buried up on Boot Hill. The one the paper says is haunting the Santa Fe right-of-way."

"I heard something about it."

"Then ask who killed her."

I hoped my distress didn't show on my face.

"Then you believe the stories about her ghost."

"No," he said, "but you asked me what it would take to convince me. And I have a personal stake in finding who killed the girl and left her on the meridian marker."

"Why?"

"It was a message," he said. "The Committee of Vigilance was formed in the early days of Dodge, before the rule of law here was firmly established. We . . . Well, we took care of things. Still should, I think."

"In an extralegal manner, I take it."

"We did what had to be done."

"And the message?"

"There are certain elements that have nothing but contempt for the way civilized people live," he said. "Whoever killed the girl and left her on the monument was expressing his contempt for justice."

Justice. It was a concept in which Calder seemed to believe, but to me it was like debating how many angels could dance on the head of a pin, or reckoning how much hay Noah would need on the ark, or algebra. Just talking about the ghost of the dead girl was making me feel odd. In truth, I hadn't felt like myself since getting out of the city jail and bumping into the frightful creature Malleus and his caravan of wagons.

A sudden and uncommon urge to drink

overwhelmed me. Normally, I drink only wine, and then only a glass or two with meals, but now I craved the stuff that Potete had shared before the performance.

I motioned for the bartender and asked for a shot of mezcal.

"You want one?" I asked Calder.

"I don't drink."

"And they let you stay in Dodge?"

The waiter brought the shot over.

"What's your interest?" I asked, raising the glass. "Is there a reward?"

"No reward."

I threw back the mezcal.

It burned like before.

"That's a bad way to do business," I managed in a raw whisper as I placed the empty glass gently on the table. "How do you hope to get paid?"

"It's not like that," he said.

"Then what's it like?"

"Nobody deserves to get their throat cut from ear to ear, especially not a little blonde girl who hadn't seen eighteen summers. She was somebody's daughter. I'd like to find who did it."

"And then what?"

"Make him stand trial."

"You have an exaggerated sense of justice, Mister Calder."

"No, Miss Wylde. I have an average sense of fairness."

Now Calder was giving me a stomachache. I know how to play most people, because they are pathetically selfish and easy to manipulate. But here Calder was, apparently sincere in his desire to do something in which he had absolutely no personal stake—and asking me to make contact with probably the only real ghost in Dodge City.

"Sorry," I said. "I can't help you."

18

As I watched Calder walk through the shadow and smoke-filled confines of the Saratoga and out the open door into the sunshine of Front Street, I felt as if a scorpion had crawled up inside my belly.

I blamed it on the mezcal.

"What's the trouble?" Bartholomew Potete asked, pulling a chair far enough out from the table to allow him to rest his bulk. "You look like you've lost your best friend."

"I have no friends."

"But you have many admirers," Potete said, pulling a stack of notes from his vest pocket. "I have a dozen invitations here for picnic lunches or carriage rides during the afternoon, a half-dozen requests for dinner, and three marriage proposals."

"Not very flattering, when you consider

the men outnumber women here a hundred to one."

"It is a seller's market," Potete said. He took a deck of playing cards from his pocket and fanned them out in front of him, then expertly tipped them back the other way. "But there is more. Because of popular demand, the opera house would like to book a return engagement of The Reverend Professor Wylde."

"When?"

Potete riffled the cards. "Tonight."

"I'm busy."

"With what?" A strip shuffle.

"A personal obligation."

"Next Monday, then? After the hearing."

"I hope to be on the train to Denver."

"Saturday," Potete suggested. "There will be a new batch of cowpunchers to charm. The *Times* reports three large herds have crossed the quarantine line in Comanche County, faced down the grangers, and are expected here tomorrow."

I shrugged.

"Wonderful," Potete growled. "I'll make all the arrangements. And I have to say, your demonstration was impressive in every regard. And playing Judge Grout that way—brilliant!"

"I am going straight to hell."

"As your lawyer, I advise you that we can beat the charge."

"You'll have to find a new shill for the billet

reading," I said. "We can't use Timothy again, but I have other work for him. I'll need him tomorrow night."

"No problem," Potete said. "Any special instructions?"

"Tell him that I am depending upon him for my safety, so he needs to stick close by. But no guns. I don't like guns and can't stand to have them around me."

"Understood."

"Any news from Counselor Sutton?" I asked.

"He has been unusually quiet," Potete said. "If he has a strategy for Monday's hearing, I can't imagine what it might be. Are you still sure we can't contact anybody from Chicago to—"

"I'm sure."

"What about that Sylvestre fellow?"

"I said I was sure."

"All right, Professor, don't bite my head off." Sulking, Potete did an overhand shuffle.

"What can you tell me about Jack Calder?"

"Nothing that will surprise you," Potete said. "With Jack, what you see is what you get. Sure, he's brighter than your average Texan, and good with that Russian on his hip. He's reading the law with Hunnicutt, hoping to go from bounty hunter to barrister. But the law would be a poor choice for Calder, because he may be the only honest man in Dodge City."

"Then what's he doing here?"

"Unlike the rest of us—who came because

we were bored, or we didn't fit in back where we came from, or we were just looking to make a quick dollar—Calder came here to make a home. Built one, too, five years back. But somebody else lives in it now."

"Why?"

"Calder said he couldn't stand living in the house, and he couldn't burn it down, so he just walked away from it and began living in a shed back of the law office."

"Why couldn't he live in it?"

"After he built it, he went back to Presidio County in Texas to fetch his wife and child, but they died somewhere along the trail."

"How?"

"Don't know. Jack doesn't talk about it."

"Did he marry again?"

Potete looked at me.

"Forget I asked."

"No, he is not married," Potete said. "Is that a good thing or a bad thing?"

"I don't know."

He placed the deck in front of me. "Cut the cards for drinks?"

"You first."

The king of spades.

"Can you beat that?"

"No," I said.

I ordered two mezcals.

We clinked our shot glasses together.

"Arriba, abajo, al centor, al dento!" Potete said,

and moved his shot glass in a curious way, up and down, as if making a blessing. Then he drank down the liquor and grimaced. *"Para todo mal mezcal, para todo bien tambien."*

For everything bad, there's mezcal.

And for everything good, there's mezcal.

19

By the time Jim Murdock came back with his homework, it was near dark and the Saratoga was roaring. I wasn't feeling too badly myself, having had three or five more mezcals in the interval. Maybe that's why I gave all of Diamond Jim's money back, except five dollars for overhead.

Jim had folded the letter neatly, in that old-fashioned way that people did before envelopes became common, and had put his sister's name on the outside in a painfully neat hand: *KATIE.*

"You get it all down?"

He nodded.

I slipped the letter into my vest.

"What now?"

"I will summon the spirits tonight," I said. "Then I will send this letter, through a sort of spiritual postal service."

"Don't you need an address?"

"Summerland has no street numbers."

He nodded. "How will I know that she received it?"

"You'll know," I said. "You'll have a warm feeling in your heart, just as if you've talked to her yourself. It may take a day or two, but it will come, and there may be some sort of sign along with it—something will remind you of the way you and Kathryn were as children, some innocent secret that you shared, and you will be able to go on with your life free from grief, knowing that your beloved sister has survived death."

He reached out and gripped my hand.

I jerked back, because I don't like people touching me, but his young hand was too strong.

"Thank you."

"For God's sake, don't cry," I said. "Not here, Jim."

Jim dabbed his eyes with his red kerchief.

"Oh, what's this?" a deep voice shouted from across the room. "Is that the famous Diamond Jim Murdock with tears in his eyes?"

I couldn't see who was saying this, because of all the cowboys at the tables around us. It was a regular orgy of gambling, drinking, and assorted riot. Jim recognized the voice, however.

"Go away, Deger!"

Actually, he didn't say "go away," he said something so coarse that I am loath to repeat it here.

"Careful, or I'll have to run you in for drunk and disorderly."

The wall of cowboys disgorged an enormous man, at least three hundred pounds, a marshal's badge pinned to his collar and a small revolver hanging from a couple of yards of cartridge belt that circled his girth. He had a mustache, which needed trimming, and he looked, for all the world, like a walrus impersonating a lawman.

"I'm not drunk," Jim said.

"Tell me it ain't so!" Deger said, walking over to the table on legs like tree stumps. "Is there no water in Jordan? No balm in Gilead? I'm surprised the sky has not fallen."

"I'm sorry," I said. "This young man and I were having a conversation."

I may have slurred that last word.

"'Conversation'?" Deger laughed. "You can't even say the word. How much whiskey have you drunk?"

"No whiskey."

"Ah," he said, a fat hand grabbing a chair and dragging it over. He turned it around and straddled it, backward, crossing his arms on top of the back. I could hear the wood protesting under the weight. "I've heard about you, the Spiritualist. What's your name? Kate Bender?"

"They have said so."

Deger waited for me to elaborate, but I disappointed.

"Aren't you going to answer?" he asked. "You are accused of many things."

"I answer to a Higher Authority."

"Well, you're not Jesus Christ, so that must mean district court."

"She's not Kate Bender," Jim blurted. "She's good and kind and—"

"Shut up, Jim," Deger said. "Or I just might run you in for public display of stupidity."

Some cowboys nearby overheard and laughed.

Jim started to rise for battle, but I placed a hand on his arm.

"Think of your sister," I said. "What would she want in this situation?"

"For me to turn the other cheek," he said, ashamed.

"Now, Marshal," I said. "Is there some business you have with me?"

"There's the matter of the city permit," he said. "I usually let my assistant marshal, Wyatt Earp, handle this sort of thing, but he's been away on business these past few months in Deadwood in the Dakota Territory."

"Ha!" Jim snorted. "Wyatt and his brother used to run a whorehouse south of the tracks on Douglas Street. Back in Wichita, Wyatt nearly shot himself in the leg when he accidently discharged his own piece. And in the Indian Territory, he was arrested for horse theft. Some lawman!"

"You have a big mouth, Jim."

"I'm just saying what everybody already knows."

"Leave us," Deger said. "I'll deal with you later."

Jim looked at me for direction.

"Go on," I said. "But remember your promise. Go straight to the depot and send that telegraph."

Deger swiveled his head to watch him go, and his fat cheeks and bulging eyes reminded me of a bulldog.

"Drink?" I asked.

"I quit drinking," Deger said. From his pocket, he took a tin of chocolates, opened it, and plucked one from the nest of wrappers. His eyes closed as he chewed.

"What about this permit?"

"The permit," he said, opening his eyes.

"I'm sure Mister Potete can take care of that."

"No," he said, still chewing. "This is not that kind of permit."

"You mean, it's not a legal permit. It's a 'shakedown,' or whatever you'd like to call it."

"I call it 'the cost of doing business,'" Deger said, then swallowed. "And it seemed like business was pretty good at the opera house the other night. I reckon about fifty dollars would make us square."

"For the whole week or just last night?"

"Just last night."

I took fifty dollars in banknotes and put them on the table.

"I expect that I'm also buying some protection for this."

"You'll have no trouble from me," Deger said, scooping up the bills.

"Partners, then."

"If you like to call it that."

"I do ask one small favor in return."

He looked at me with his bulldog eyes.

"If a man by the name of Armbruster comes inquiring after me, you are to get me word quickly and quietly. No, don't ask—better you don't know. But you'll remember the name, right?"

"I'll remember," Deger said.

Then there was the sound of dogs yapping and through the legs of the cowboys ran a trio of coonhounds, followed by a small man in white britches and high hunting boots. And when I say "small," I mean *small*. He must not have been more than five-two, even in the boots, and his overall impression was that of a child playing dress-up.

Beside the small fellow was a full-sized man with a humorless expression. His hands were clasped in front of him.

"Mayor," Deger said with ice in his voice.

"Marshal," the small man answered with equal venom.

The hounds were creating general chaos underfoot.

"I've got to go," Deger said, rising from the chair.

"Don't you like dogs?" I asked.

"Not all of 'em," Deger said over his shoulder as he huffed away.

"James Kelley," the small man said, extending his hand to me. "But most folks around here call me 'Dog.'"

When I clasped his hand, he bent down and kissed the back of mine.

I tried to keep from laughing.

"This here is Hoodoo Brown," Kelley said, motioning to the dour man.

"The same Hoodoo Brown I've read about in the local paper?"

"Yes, ma'am."

"Where'd you get that curious handle of 'Hoodoo'?"

"It's jes' my name."

"Mister Brown is a mite bashful about his powers," Kelley said. "But he is one of the finest conjure men there is. He grew up in Missouri and learned it from his old uncle Ben, who taught him to use the Good Book to cast spells. Some say that his skill with a long gun comes from a certain passage in Genesis."

"Hesh up, Dog."

"We're here to talk to you about the ghost of the murdered girl," Kelley said.

"Sit down, gentlemen," I said.

They did.

"We'd like to know if you'd come out and talk to the ghost tonight," Kelley said. "You know, ask her what her name is and what she wants."

"Get right to the point, in other words."

"That's it exactly," Dog said. "What a mystery! It's been driving me mad."

"Oh, I'm sure it's not the only thing," I said, pushing one of the coondogs off my lap. "Hoodoo, is the account in the paper true? You saw the apparition?"

"I did," he said.

"Blonde hair? Taffeta dress?"

"Not taffeta," he said. "Nothing so fancy. Calico."

"Ah, yes," I said. "And the strange light?"

"It was not as the *Times* described it," he said. "It wasn't a spotlight. It was more of a soft bluish glow, like very bright moonlight. The whole affair has upset my digestion and disturbed my sleep."

"Ghosts tend to have that effect," I said.

"I'd like to be able to eat without distress, and to sleep the night again," he said.

"Understandable," I said.

"So you will challenge the specter?"

"Gentlemen," I said. "I've had some experience in these affairs, as you might imagine. I must warn you that confronting the ghost might not have the hoped-for result. Something a bit gentler might produce a more beneficial result."

"'Gentler'?" Brown asked.

"A séance," Kelley said.

I nodded.

"When?" Brown asked.

"Tomorrow night," I said. "I have an engagement at the opera house, but there will be time after. Please call upon me at the Dodge House just before midnight."

"Delighted," Kelley said.

"There will be some small charge for my services."

"Only fair," Kelley said. "Because this is a matter of civic interest, I will take the funds from petty cash. How much should I bring?"

"Fifty dollars. Now, if I might ask a question."

"You may ask me anything," Kelley said.

"Why is there an empty grave up on Boot Hill?"

"Two weeks ago, we buried a ranger by the name of Powers, who was shot to death in a dance hall on the south side," he said. "We didn't know anything about him except his name. But his people in Ellsworth read about his demise and came, dug him up, and threw him in a wagon to take home to the family plot."

"And they left a shovel and an open grave?"

The little mayor shrugged.

"I believe it was meant as a sort of editorial comment on our city," he said. "And I must admit, we have seen more than our share of violent death. In the first year alone, fifteen men killed on the streets of Dodge or in her dance halls and saloons. We have been described by the Eastern papers as 'the most wicked town in the West.' Now, these fainthearted editors mean that as a criticism, but I take it as a compliment. Find something you're good at, I always say, and stick with it."

They left, and the dogs followed.

I had one more mezcal.

When I stood, the floor of the Saratoga seemed tilted at a crazy angle. But I threaded my way through the clot of cowboys to the outside, even if my legs seemed a bit heavy.

It was a cool night, heavy with the smell of rain. Overhead, a layer of clouds hid the stars. Far beyond town, a coyote howled. Or was it a wolf?

I took the cigar from my pocket and bit off one end. Then I jammed the Key West in the corner of my mouth. A passing cowboy paused, struck a match with his thumb, then cupped his hands around the flame. I pulled Diamond Jim's letter from my vest and held it to the cowboy's match, setting one corner on fire.

"Thanks," I said.

I waited until the letter was fully ablaze before using it to light the cigar.

20

I woke just before noon in my bed at the Dodge House, with my head throbbing like somebody had beaten me over the head with a shovel. My hair stank of cigar smoke and my mouth tasted like the floor of the Saratoga.

"Oh, Eddie," I moaned, sitting up and resting my forehead on my knees. "What have I done?"

"'Nevermore!'"

"Never," I vowed. "I'm *never* drinking again."

Then I remembered I had a performance that night, to be followed by a séance with some less-than-charming Dodge City types, and I threw myself back on the pillows.

I thought I saw Horrible Hank leering at me from the mirror on the wall.

"Perfect," I said. "Join the party."

I forced myself to pull on some clothes, stumble downstairs, and walk down Front Street in search of a chemist. On my way, I passed Beatty & Kelley Restaurant, and just the smell of the bacon and fried eggs nearly brought me to my knees. I found the City Drug, on the west side of the Saratoga.

"What's the matter?"

"I'm in distress," I said, leaning against the counter.

"Well, come on over here and sit down before you fall over," a man of about thirty with thick spectacles and a halo of sandy hair said. He helped me to a padded chair near the back.

He placed a hand on my stomach. "How far along are you?"

I swatted his hand away. "I'm not with child! I'm hungover."

"Apologies," the man said. "But when most women say they are 'in distress,' it typically means they are pregnant."

"I'm not most women," I said. "Just tell me what you have to relieve the pounding in my head."

"What kind of pounding?" he asked, placing a hand on my temple and tilting my head back to peer into my pupils. "Did you fall, or were you beaten, or did you indulge in too many spirits?"

I again brushed his hand away. "What is wrong with you?"

"I'm a doctor."

"Well, I don't like to be touched. Restrain yourself."

"As you wish."

"Are you a real doctor or a conjure man or just another frontier quack?"

"Pain makes people unpleasant, doesn't it?" He was still smiling. "Oh, I reckon I'm a real-enough doctor for Dodge. I studied in Philadelphia, then practiced in St. Louis for a couple of years. Was on my way to Denver when I stopped over in Dodge City to see my brother-in-law and have been here ever since. There was a need, you know."

"So you get what Boot Hill doesn't?"

"I'd rather think it is the other way around. I do as much as is humanly possible, but sometimes there's no way to keep body and spirit together," he said. "I've set broken bones, healed burns, and mined more than my share of lead from the slow and the unlucky."

He said his name was Thomas McCarty. He moved behind the counter and studied his shelves of bottles and boxes.

"I wouldn't argue," I said. "But there's something else."

He looked at me with raised eyebrows.

"I'm not myself," I said. "I'm doing things I wouldn't do otherwise. This drinking binge, for instance. Never done that before."

"Always a first time."

"I hope it is the *only* time."

"Now, the old-timers say the best cure for the common hangover is to brew up some tea using rabbit pellets," Doc McCarty said, lifting his glasses so he could read the label on a small tin he had taken from the shelf. "You could try some rabbit-drop tea, if you like."

"The thought makes me want to hurt you."

"Here, I have something that will relieve the headache," McCarty said. "Don't worry, this won't turn you into a hoppie or a laudanum whore. It's a powder that is mostly caffeine."

"Why not just drink coffee?"

"Because you'd have to drink a whole pot of it," he said. "Dissolve a teaspoon of this in a glass of water and drink it down. Then drink three or four more glasses of water after that, because part of the pain of a hangover is dehydration."

"What irony."

Doc McCarty got a glass and filled it with water from a pitcher behind the counter.

"I'd avoid the water at most of these joints along Front Street," he said as he spooned the powder into the glass, then mixed it vigorously. "Mostly, they go down to the Arkansas River and fill their buckets. Problem is, there are a few thousand longhorns in the fields around us. When these beasts eliminate, their product trickles into the river."

He handed me the glass. "This water comes from my rain barrel out back."

I muttered my thanks. Then I drank down half the glass.

Then Doc McCarty fetched a bottle of

bourbon from a cabinet, walked over, and uncorked it.

"You can't be serious," I said, covering the glass with my hand. "Just the smell of it makes me want to retch."

"Just an ounce or two," he said. "You're suffering alcohol withdrawal. A bit will ease the pain."

I moved my hand.

"So much for *never*."

He poured a shot into the water, turning it the color of weak tea. "You're that woman, aren't you?"

"What woman?"

"Professor Wylde, the medium."

"Uh-huh," I said, drinking the watered-down bourbon.

"I would be interested in doing an investigation of your powers."

"No thanks," I said. "I've been subjected to enough at the hands of educated men. They have done things to me during séances that wouldn't have been allowed during the Inquisition."

"What do you mean?"

"It begins simply enough, with the doctors wanting to hold your hands to make sure that you're not manipulating objects. Then it progresses to the binding of both the hands and the feet, and of the legs. Sometimes they will tie your hands behind your back and then run a cord from that to your ankles. And then there are the searches, being required to shed every piece of clothing to assure them that you're not hiding some apparatus for making fraud inside your bloomers, and then they want to examine your mouth and other orifices. Finally you are put in stocks, or your entire body is locked inside a box with holes for just your hands, and barely enough room to breathe."

"Sounds unpleasant," Doc McCarty said.

"That's like calling an iron maiden uncomfortable," I said. "The medical doctors will never accept communication with the dead, even if Jesus Christ appeared before them Himself and told them what Ben Franklin had for lunch in Summerland and where Captain Kidd hid all the loot."

Doc McCarty smiled.

"Well, I wasn't planning to bring out the thumbscrews," he said. "I'm just curious, that's all. I've seen enough to know there are more things in heaven and earth—people surviving wounds that should have killed them, prayer making a difference, folks coming back from being a few minutes dead and talking about bright lights and dead relatives."

"You sound like a regular sky pilot, Doc."

"Faith is not unusual," he said. "It's the natural condition of man. But it's curious that a woman who professes to demonstrate spirit communication seems skeptical of religious faith. Don't you believe, Miss Wylde?"

"I believed in a lot of things, Doc," I said, "when I was a child. But now, I have given up childish things."

"That's good," he said. "Using the Bible to support your disbelief. Clever."

"Glad you liked it," I said.

"But clever never eased an aching heart."

"You're selling clever short, Doc." I handed him the empty glass. "You're onto something with this headache powder and bourbon cure," I said. "You could patent it and make a fortune. I can almost hear myself think again."

The front door opened with a bang.

Jack Calder backed into the drugstore, carrying a man by the legs, two dusty cowboy boots sticking out beneath each elbow. Tom the Jailer, had the other half, and between them was a thin orso covered in blood. The man's head bobbed limply against Tom's stomach.

"Over here," Doc McCarty said as he cleared a table of a coal oil lamp and a few books. The body was deposited on the table, and Doc McCarty ripped open the bloody shirt.

There was a ragged hole in the man's chest, about the diameter of a coffee can. The edges of the skin were blackened, and, deep inside, I could see white splinters of his sternum—and beneath that, his beating heart.

Doc splattered whiskey over his hands, handed off the bottle, and rubbed them together with vigor. Then he plunged both hands into the wound, attempting to stop the bleeding.

The stricken man's eyes shot open and he uttered a terrible gasp.

I realized the man was the bullwhacker whom I had seen with the freight caravan during my first day in Dodge.

"What happened?" Doc asked.

"Don't know," Calder said. "Found him like this on the south bank of the Arkansas River."

"Get her out of here," Doc snapped.

"Let me stay," I said. "I recognize the man."

"What do you want us to do, Doc?" Calder asked.

"I—I don't know," Doc McCarty stammered. "I've never seen a wound like this. It's as if he was shot in the chest with a mountain howitzer, but there's no ball or shot or any fragments."

The bullwhacker turned his head. His eyes rolled, and a stream of blood poured from the corner of his mouth to puddle on the floor. There was a hollow rush of air as his lungs emptied.

"He's gone," Doc said.

"No more chipped beef for him," Tom said.

"Show some respect," Doc said. "Take off your hat, at least."

Doc slowly removed his hands from the man's chest. As he did, he drew out a sliver of something that looked like glass. In bloody fingers, Doc held the shard up to the light to get a better look at it.

Red and black swirled and coiled.

"It looks like a chip from a shattered marble," Doc said.

Then the piece evaporated, leaving Doc holding nothing.

A shiver ran down my spine as I remembered Malleus and his leather bag and the violet-and-yellow-and-blue marble he had plucked from the mud after knocking the wind from me.

"What was that?" Tom the Jailer asked.

"Never saw anything like it," Doc said.

"It was a splintered aura," I said.

"What?" Calder asked.

"An aura is a shadow your soul casts," I said. "But that one wasn't his. It was somebody else's. It was somehow shot into his chest, like a bullet, where it exploded."

"That's the craziest thing I ever heard," Calder said.

"You said you knew this man?" Doc asked.

"No, but I've seen him," I said. "He drove the oxen for Malleus, the repulsive creature who owns the freight company. I don't remember the bullwhacker's name."

"Shadrach," Calder said.

"Yes, that's it."

"Malleus, you say?" Doc asked. "What an odd name."

"What language is that?" Calder asked.

"A dead one," Doc said. "A *'malleus'* is Latin for 'hammer,' and the reason I know is because I had to learn it in medical school. It's the name of a small bone in the ear that transmits sound vibrations from the eardrum."

"Where did you meet this Malleus?" Calder asked.

"On Bridge Street," I said. "The freight caravan was coming back into town from someplace in Texas. On Wednesday, I think. They had a problem with a wheel and Malleus bumped into me. It was unpleasant. There was also a handsome man who rode with them, a whiskey trader."

"Vanderslice," Calder said with venom.

"He did not tell me his name."

"What color was his shirt?"

"Black, with mother-of-pearl buttons."

"That's Vanderslice," Calder said. "He's a bad type. I received a federal warrant for his arrest this morning. He's been selling liquor to the Indians."

"Then why don't you arrest him?"

"I would, but he left yesterday with the freight wagon train to Fort Elliott. He travels with the train nearly to the Canadian, then breaks off and heads west, toward a hideout nobody's ever seen. Rumor is that he keeps a Comanche wife and child there."

Doc McCarty threw a sheet over the body.

"Sorry you had to witness that," he told me.

I mumbled something and stepped out of the drugstore to Front Street.

Using the technique of looking while not looking, which Jonathan had first taught me so long ago, I scanned the people around me: cowboys with red or yellow auras, businessmen with hues that ranged from green to tan, a few working girls who were out early and whose auras ran the gamut, including some blacks and orange.

Then I looked at myself in a shop window.

Nothing. No violet, no yellow, no blue.

I no longer had an aura.

This creature, this Malleus, had stolen my aura and trapped it in a leather bag, along with the rest of his collection, and was now somewhere on the southern plains.

The thought made me sick.

I fell to my knees there in the mud and heaved until nothing more would come up.

21

"I am Kate Bender and I address you from hell."

The voice was cold and proud and had some foreign accent, but not German. Greek, perhaps. I was aware that the words were coming from me, and I knew I was standing on the stage of the opera house, but I was asleep.

The question that had preceded the trance—"Are you Kate Bender?"—had come near the end of the performance, but there were still a few minutes of candle left, so I had to give some kind of answer. There are, of course, a thousand ways of replying without answering. I was just about to launch into one of those long-winded, but meaningless, monologues, when I involuntarily uttered a single word: "Yes."

I had never heard a crowd go so quiet.

Fils de salope, I thought. What was wrong with me? Was it still the aftereffects of the hangover?

Did losing my aura also make me stupid? I cursed myself and prepared another tack, this one about how we really were all Kate Bender, because there lurks the capacity for great evil in all of us. It was then I slipped into the trance and began talking with this voice that was not my own.

"Now we're getting somewhere," the cowboy with the auburn curls, who had come back for the repeat performance, declared. "Tell us, Kate Bender, how did you and your murderous kin escape?"

"Magic," the voice said. "Only magic. How else could this supposed family, the four most wanted people in America, disappear without a trace?"

The fingers of my left hand moved up and unbuttoned my vest.

"What kind of magic?" the cowboy asked.

"The forbidden kind," the voice said.

My fingers now unbuttoned the top of my blouse and spread the collar, exposing some cleavage. Strangely, the cowboys were quiet. Then my hands pulled out my shirttail and smoothed it over my pants.

"Can you tell us why you killed all those people? Was it for the money?"

"The money?" the voice asked. "What fool kills for money? There is only one reason for murder, and that is for power. Our master required human blood, and we gave it to him, by the bucketful."

"Ask another question," somebody urged the cowboy with the curls.

"All right," he said, less confident now. "Do you serve Satan?"

"It is easier to name those who don't," the voice said.

"Tell Old Scratch to go on down to the Saratoga," somebody called. "Old Chalk Beeson'll serve anybody!"

This got some laughs.

"You are amused," the voice said. Now my fingers were fussing with my hair, smoothing it over one ear. "But the one I serve walks among you, like a wolf among lambs. He is the hammer that will pound the stob of man down beyond the ground. From the world of darkness, he hath loosed devils and demons. He maketh me to lie down with putrefaction, and he hath led us down the paths of wickedness for damnation's sake."

My back arched and my shoulders spread as if I had wings.

"The master bade us become pioneers," the voice said. "Pioneers of a new kind of evil, a random and serial evil, an evil that will make people distrust their neighbors while at the same time creating an obscene craving for every detail of depravity."

I felt my face grow tight with a smile.

"You want to know, don't you?" the voice asked. "What does it feel like to drive a hammer into a man's skull, to feel that terrible weight

bury itself in flesh and brain and bone? Would
you like me to share the ecstasy of that first
splash of warm blood, the smell of copper and
salt, the thrill of squashing a human life as you
would squash a bug in your hand?"

My left fist was clenched tightly in front of me.

"Of course, you would," the voice said.

The smile changed to a leer. My hands cupped
my breasts and then went down my sides to
my hips.

"This body—so like mine was. You find it
pleasing, no?"

Nobody answered.

"Cowards," the voice taunted.

The feet carried me to the edge of the stage.
"You!"

My finger jabbed at the cowboy with the
auburn curls. "'Come here and touch this body
and connect with my soul. Feel what men have
died for. Die yourself, in the fire of my em-
brace.'"

The cowboy didn't move.

"Fool," the voice sneered. "I offer you the
chance to commit one great unholy act, to be
consumed by a passion you did not know existed, to have your name writ large beside mine
in the nightmares of mortals, and you sit with
your hands crossed over your member like a
frightened schoolboy."

My finger admonished all of them, trailing
a bit of flame from the tip.

"You are nothing," the voice said. "All of

you—nothing. In a few short years, you will be in the ground. In a few years after that, everyone who knew you will lie in silent graves as well. Who will remember any of you? It will be as if you never existed. But in a hundred years, the name 'Kate Bender' will still burn on living tongues!"

The candle flame shuddered and went out. Then my eyes rolled back to show only whites, my body shook, and I collapsed on the stage.

22

Sitting cross-legged on my uncomfortable bed in the Dodge House, I was feeling very sorry for myself. I looked at my aura-less image in the mirror above the dresser. Never had I looked older. There were dark circles under my eyes, wrinkles, and crow's-feet. My complexion was even more pale than usual. The image that stared back at me was not that of a twenty-eight-year-old woman but that of a crone.

Save for my image, the mirror was empty.

Not even Horrible Hank was interested.

Silent tears stained my cheeks.

I didn't know if I had really become a channel for the damned Kate Bender, or whether the loss of my aura had made me susceptible to some meddlesome spirit, or whether I was just sinking ever deeper into insanity.

It all made me want to drink a barrel of mezcal.

* * *

Sometimes, I just wanted someone to talk to.

Then came a knock on the door.

"Just a moment," I called, wiping away my tears with a handkerchief embroidered with Jonathan's initials.

"Well, Eddie," I said quietly. "It seems that I am coming apart. You might be wise to find a new mistress, or there might not be any more bread crumbs or raisins or treats of beef jerky for you. What do you think of that?"

Eddie shifted his head to look at me with first one eye and then the other, but he voiced no opinion.

"All right," I said. "We'll play this one straight, just for once."

I climbed down from the bed and didn't even bother to arrange myself before opening the door. There stood Dog Kelley and Hoodoo Brown. Kelley appeared to be dressed in the same foxhunting getup he had worn the other day, and three hounds serpentined underfoot.

"Professor," Kelley said, removing his top hat with a sweeping gesture as if he were addressing a duchess. "We have come at the appointed hour. I trust we are expected?"

"Of course, Mayor," I said. "But I beg you to leave your dogs in the hall or, better yet, downstairs. Dogs make my raven nervous, and it would not be conducive to a good session."

"But I go everywhere with the hounds."

"Please," I said. "There can be no séance with canine tumult."

"Very well," he said, and sulked. "Hoodoo, would you take the boys downstairs and have the night man watch after them?"

Brown knelt down, petted each dog on the head and around the ears, and then took off down the hall, with the dogs bounding after him.

"Come in," I said.

"You have the best rooms in the city."

"That is sad," I said. "The wind blows the dust through the walls."

"One becomes used to it."

"Not this one," I said tiredly.

We walked over to a round table in the corner, not far from Eddie's cage, and I motioned for Kelley to sit. He did, and then removed fifty dollars in gold from his vest pocket. He placed the coins on the table.

I picked up the money and felt its weight.

"Is there any charity in Dodge City?" I asked.

"Of the biblical kind, madam?"

"I mean of the widows-and-orphans kind," I said. "Has there been a fund established to help the less fortunate, or to feed the hungry, or to do any other kind of work to relieve human suffering?"

Kelley thought a moment.

"There's the sanitary committee," he said. "Doctors McCarty and Galland head it up. They are always harping on the need to establish a hospital here in town, rather than being required to send the desperately ill five miles out to the infirmary at Fort Dodge."

"Then I want to be an anonymous donor to that committee," I said, and pushed the money back to him. "See that Doc McCarty receives it for the purpose stated. And, Mayor, I expect to read about that donation in the next edition of the *Times*."

"Of course," he said, scooping up the coins. "I will deliver it to Doctor McCarty the first thing in the morning."

I had left the door ajar and Hoodoo Brown walked in, followed by Timothy, my polite tramp.

"You're late," I told Timothy.

He put his hands together beneath his chin, begging forgiveness. Then he made a motion as if dealing cards.

"You'll lose all your money," I told him, and he gave me a look that said, *Well, hey, I don't need money. I'm a tramp.*

Brown and Timothy took their seats at the table.

I went around the room, blowing out the lamps, and came back with a lit white candle in a brass holder. I placed the candle in the center of the table and took a deep breath; then I looked at the faces of the men around me. It had been a long time since I had conducted a session in earnest.

"Does anyone have the time?"

Brown opened his pocket watch.

"Five minutes after midnight."

I nodded.

"It is Sunday, the Thirteenth of May," I said. "We will attempt two spirit communications this morning. The first will be to contact the ghost of the girl who walks the railroad right-of-way. In the second, we will endeavor to contact the spirit of Jonathan Wylde, my forever-young husband, killed on this day, thirteen years ago."

Kelley and Brown made some small sympathetic remarks, which I ignored.

"Now there are a few rules to discuss," I said. "Once we touch hands, we cannot let go, no matter what happens. To do so is to break the bond of trust we have established. If an apparition appears, you may ask questions, but expect the answers to be circular or nonsensical, as ghosts are obsessed with their own unfinished business. Understood?"

The men nodded their understanding.

"Let us join hands."

We clasped each other's hands. This was unpleasant for me, with Dog Kelley on one side and Hoodoo Brown on the other. As I've told you, I don't like to be touched. Kelley's hand was soft and sweaty, but Brown's was rough, like burlap.

We concentrated on the candle flame.

By and by, everything became very still, and even Eddie stopped fidgeting around in his cage.

"This is Ophelia Wylde," I said in a soothing

voice. "I am here with some earnest men from Dodge City who wish to contact the spirit of the girl slain on the meridian marker. Can you show us some sign that you are with us?"

The candle flame rippled, as if we might have some success.

But then, nothing.

For another half hour, we tried. I kept up the appeals to the spirit of the dead girl, but nothing came through. Finally, admitting defeat, I brought the first portion of the session to a close.

"Let us take a short break," I said.

We unclasped our hands and rubbed them to restore circulation.

"That was disappointing," Kelley said.

"It often is," I said. "But the spirits choose their own time and place to appear. Are we ready for the second half?"

We clasped hands again, and this time we spent a longer time staring into the candle flame. I was reluctant to begin, knowing that this was the last time I would attempt to contact my lost husband.

"Jonathan," I said at last. "It's me, Ophelia."

The flame did not waver.

"Today is the thirteenth anniversary of your death, and I so would like to make contact with you. Do you remember what you used to tell me, that love survives death? I'm asking now, for the last time, for you to send proof from the other side. We had a secret message. Do you remember? Could you communicate that to one of these men?"

Silence in the room.

Cowboys howled along Front Street.

Coyotes cried at the edge of town.

"I miss you so much," I said. "We were so young, and we had so little time together. And I was so much in love with you! You were so naïve. And how I came to resent that naivety, to hate how you went to that damned war and left me all alone, forever."

I was weeping, again.

"Not knowing how you died has haunted me," I said. "It would be such a comfort just to know of your last few minutes, to know what comrades surrounded you, to learn what you said with your last breath there in the trenches at Spottsylvania."

At this, Brown squeezed my hand tightly.

"What I wouldn't give to touch your cheek one more time," I said. "What I have tried to give to touch your cheek one more time. Oh, Jonathan, if only you knew, you would be so ashamed. I have been so weak with loss for so many years. I have lost the path. I mourn for the life we should have had. I ache with the thought of our children unborn. I am alone, Jonathan— a woman alone."

I had not cried so in years.

A bubble of snot clung to one of my nostrils, but I kept my grip.

"Nothing, Jonathan?" I asked. "No sign?"

The men were staring at their laps, afraid to look at me.

"Very well," I said, sniffling. "I still miss you more than I ever thought it possible to miss another human being. I have tried everything within my power to reach you, but to no effect. I hope that we will meet again, in Summerland or whatever the hereafter might be called, but I don't think there's such a place. But I will say a prayer each night that I am wrong."

I released the hands on either side of me.

"Thank you, gentlemen," I said. "This ends our session."

"We should stay for just a few minutes," Brown said.

"Careful, Mister Brown, or somebody just might mistake you for a gentleman," I said. Then I buried my face in a handkerchief and blew my nose. "Truly, I'll be fine. I apologize that the session was unproductive."

Kelley and Brown left, and then I urged Timothy to depart as well.

"Go," I said, "I just need to get some sleep."

He shook his head and indicated he would sit at the table while I slept.

"How in the world am I supposed to sleep with a man hovering over me?" I asked. "Thank you for your kindness, but for the last time, go."

I shut the door behind him and turned to Eddie.

"Well, I guess that's that," I said. "What do you think we should do for the next thirteen years?"

23

I couldn't sleep.

At two o'clock I got up, pulled on my clothes, and walked downstairs. Dodge City was still rolling from the momentum of Saturday night. Every joint along both Front Streets was lit up like Nero's Rome. Everywhere was laughter and shouts and cowboy music. In the shadows between the buildings, rough men and easy women made furtive bargains. Over it all, the leaden disk of a new moon hung in the southwest like a cipher.

I shouldered my way into the Saratoga and headed for the bar. In the corner, some half-drunk cowpuncher was strumming a guitar and singing: *"As I rode down by Tom Sherman's barroom, Tom Sherman's barroom so early one day."*

The bartender smiled and asked if I wanted a mezcal.

"Thanks, but no," I said.

"*There I spied a handsome young ranger, all wrapped in white linen, as cold as the clay.*"

"Whiskey?" the bartender asked.

"Do you have any tea?"

"*I see by your outfit that you are a ranger, come sit down beside me and hear my sad story. I'm shot through the breast and know I must die.*"

The bartender frowned.

"We have coffee. That's what Chalkley drinks, mostly."

"No, I want tea. Hot tea."

"Like the English drink?"

"Exactly. No whiskey, no coffee, no mezcal. Tea."

"*Then muffle the drums and play the dead marches, play the dead march as I'm carried along.*"

"We have the stuff we pour for the girls when they're sitting at the tables, so they don't get roaring drunk," the bartender said. "It's tea, I think, but it was brewed yesterday afternoon, maybe."

"*Take me to the churchyard and lay the sod o'er me.*"

"How perfectly horrid," I said.

"*I'm a young ranger and I know I've done wrong.*"

"It's not such a bad song," the bartender said.

"I wasn't talking about the song," I said. "The words are new, but the tune is an old one. I heard it growing up in Memphis and later in New Orleans."

I thanked the bartender and left the Saratoga, bound for the City Drug, thinking that perhaps

Doc McCarty might still be at his station, since nobody in Dodge City seemed to sleep. If I could find some proper English tea anywhere, I thought, it ought to be there.

But before I reached the drugstore, a familiar voice called to me from the shadows between buildings.

"Katie."

I paused.

"Diamond Jim?" I asked.

"Come here, I want to talk to you."

"Have you been drinking, Jim?"

I peered into the darkness. I could see the outline of Jim Murdock and two others. A bottle was being passed among them. Jim took the bottle and took a long pull before handing it off.

"That's not going to please your folks," I said. "Did you contact them, like I asked?"

"Sure did," he said. "Telegraphed them right away, just like you said, after I gave you that letter to my sister. My *dead* sister."

His manner was oddly aggressive.

"Let's talk about this tomorrow," I said.

I turned, but Jim's hand shot out and grasped my right wrist.

"What are you doing?"

He pulled me into the darkness.

I screamed, but there was so much noise on Front Street already that I doubt anybody heard it. Then he clamped a hand over my mouth and put his face so close to mine that I could feel the heat from his flushed cheeks.

"You played me for a sucker," Jim said.

I tried to pull away, but Jim's friends stepped closer, their thighs pressing against me.

"Oh, you know what I'm talking about," he said. "You're nothing but a fraud. A damned fraud. Do you know what kind of telegram I got back from my folks in Ohio?"

I tried to shake my head.

"Of course, you don't," he said. "You got no powers."

His friends laughed. I was having trouble breathing.

"The telegram said my sister, Katie, was alive," Jim said. "The newspapers got it wrong when they listed her among the dead, because she was identified by the necklace. But she had given the necklace to her best friend to wear. They were sitting side by side when the train plunged into the Ashtabula River. My sister was hurt bad, and was in the hospital and unable to talk for weeks, but she survived. And that means you lied."

He removed his hand and I gulped in air.

"Jim," I said. "It wasn't like that."

"Then tell me how it was like."

"I was trying to help you."

"You have a funny way of helping people. You took my money."

"I only kept five bucks," I said. "I'll give you the money back, Jim, but please let me go."

"I don't want your money," he said.

"Then what do you want?" I asked. At this point, I was expecting to be raped.

"To teach you a lesson," he said.

One of his friends picked me up by the waist, while the other jammed my feet in a burlap sack. I started swinging my fists as hard as I could, but Jim caught my hands and cinched my wrists together with latigo. He pulled off his red kerchief and stuffed it into my mouth, to muffle my shouts. They pushed me down in the sack, pulled it over my head, and tied the end shut with a length of rope.

Then one of them slung the sack over his shoulder, with my stomach over his shoulder and my head down. I could feel each footstep in my breastbone as he carried me away from Front Street.

I was now certain that after they raped me, they would murder me. Strangely, I wasn't frightened—but I was royally pissed. I wriggled and kicked and spat the wad of kerchief from my mouth.

"Putain!" I shouted. "Put me down right now or you all are going to be sorry you were ever born. I don't like guns, but I don't mind rocks. Come morning, I'm going to find each of you and take a stone about the size of a baseball

and hit you so hard in your sensitive parts that you'll be singing soprano in the saddle."

"Jim, she sure does talk," the one carrying me said.

"We'll see how much she talks when we throw her in," Jim said.

I stopped struggling.

"What?" I asked.

We kept walking.

I began imagining all the places they could throw me.

The river, barrels, wells.

"Jim, where are you taking me?"

"Shut up."

Basements, cellars, closets.

"Really, Jim. This is not something you want to do. It's kidnapping, and there are laws against that, even in Dodge City."

"It's what you deserve, you bitch fraud."

Caves, crevices . . . holes in the ground.

Then I could feel the man carrying me was walking uphill, and I could hear the sound of gravel skittering with each step.

The open grave on Boot Hill.

Now I was frightened. No, I was terrified.

I squirmed and wriggled as hard as I could, but I had no leverage and the man holding me was just too strong.

"You other two," I said, "you'll be hanged for kidnap and murder, along with Diamond Jim. Is that what you want? All you have to do is let me go and I won't say a thing."

The man carrying me laughed.

"Ain't nobody ever hanged for killing a whore," he said, his voice as cold as ice on a winter pond. "And that's all you are—a bit higher priced than the ones in the cribs along South Front, but a whore just the same."

"What about you, the other one?" I asked. "Please, you can't let them do this. I'm not a whore! I'm a woman, just like your mother, or your sister, or your wife."

"You is not like them at all," the other man said drunkenly. "You maybe isn't a whore, but you is for damn sure a witch. I seen you at the opera house once and twice and knows you is a witch, and the Book says not to suffer a witch to live."

"But it also says a lot of other stuff," I pleaded. "Jesus said to turn the other cheek, to go and sin no more, to love thy neighbor as thyself. Don't just take the part that justifies murdering somebody."

"Daddy readed me the Book. But him died afore we got past Numbers."

We stopped walking.

"Here we are," Diamond Jim said.

"Please, Jim. No."

"I've heard about all from you I ever want to," Jim said.

"Don't bury me alive."

"Shut your mouth, witch."

"Shoot me," I pleaded. "Please shoot me. Then you can toss me in. Just make sure I'm dead first. A bullet in the head. I won't struggle or say another word, I promise. And I'll die quiet."

The man carrying me shifted my weight from his shoulder to his arms, hugging me to his chest like he would a child.

"See, I'm being good. Shoot me now. Do it quick."

The man took a step forward.

"You don't understand."

I could feel his arms tense, ready for the throw.

"I'm afraid of the dark."

24

It seemed like it took a long time for me to hit the bottom of the grave, as if I were falling from a mountaintop. I know it was just a trick of the mind, like when you drop a plate and you watch it falling slowly. You can't react quickly enough to catch it and keep it from shattering.

And I shattered when I hit bottom.

A thousand things shot through my mind at once: Was the rattlesnake I saw earlier down in the grave with me? Was any part of the exhumed gambler from Ellsworth left behind? Would I die of suffocation first or of fright? Would I, too, become a ghost that walked the streets of Dodge City? Were there any bugs or scorpions in the dirt that was raining down in clods? How long would it take for my flesh to fall from my bones? Would I stink much, and for how long? Would I get a hand-lettered wooden marker like the rest?

What would the *Dodge City Times* write about me?
Was there anybody left in Memphis or in New
Orleans who would even know who I was? Did
Tanté Marie still live? Would Paschal's widow
ever forgive him or me? Would Potter Palmer be
saddened by the news of my death, or would he
rejoice? Would the bacon baron in Louisville
give Diamond Jim the thousand dollars for
killing me? Would Michael Sutton claim that
Kate Bender had finally been dealt justice?

And, at the same instant as the rest of it,
came the most troubling thought of all: What
would become of Eddie?

Knowing you're about to die isn't like what
you read about in novels, or at least it wasn't for
me. I had no urge to confess my sins or appeal
to God or any other foolish thing. What I wanted
most was for it to be over. I hated the darkness
and the rasp of burlap and the growing weight
of dirt above me. Things became very close
there in the sack. I was turned over on my left
side, with my knees up and my hands near my
face. I covered my mouth and nose so that I
wouldn't be eating any dirt or burlap when
the end came. It was cold there at the bottom
of the grave, so cold that I began to shiver un-
controllably.

I thought about the warm night sky, arching
above me. Just knowing it was up above made
me even more miserable. If only I could have
one lungful of that night air, I would have been
eternally grateful. Then came a keen desire to

turn over, to lie on my right side. But of course, there was too much dirt pressing down on me to allow me to move even an inch.

There were so many things I had taken for granted, and now they all had been taken away by a drunken kid, who had buried me alive. That thought made me furious, and the anger was something hard and bright. I fought with elbows and knees against the inevitable. I felt like a child whose arms and legs were being held by her mother to stop a tantrum, but the smothering grave won. After a few minutes, I was exhausted and realized I was using up any air I had left.

My face was dewy with sweat, but I was colder than ever.

By and by, my teeth stopped chattering. It wasn't that I felt warm, exactly, but that I was ceasing to feel *anything*.

My mind began to drift. I forgot that I was furious. . . .

In my mind, it was no longer spring above me, but deep winter. I saw snow covering Boot Hill and Dodge City below it, and the sky was the color of the lead type used at the *Times*. All the doors and windows of the saloons and hotels and brothels were shut tight. Not a soul moved on either Front Street, and the sun dipped low in the sky. Eventually a single wolf loped into town. His hard eyes shone and his bright tongue dangled over a row of ivory teeth. His head was low to the ground and swung slyly from side to side. Behind, his tracks stitched the snow from the railroad and across the bridge and wound far below the Arkansas.

Then the wolf lunged and his teeth snapped and he caught a crow in his mouth, ruby blood splattering and black feathers floating down to the snow. I gave out a cry and was surprised to find myself back in the grave.

I was back for only a moment, however, and the darkness came down around me like a curtain.

It was as if the darkness had separated my soul from my body, but my soul was reluctant to leave and lingered nearby.

"Who is there?" a girl's voice said in Russian.

Now, I don't speak Russian, but I could understand every word. The voice was fine and young, and filled with sadness. I asked who was calling out in the darkness.

"Is that you, Andrei? Oh, Andy, where have you gone?"

I'm not Andy.

"Andrei, I don't understand. I've been so alone. Are you coming back?"

Tell me your name.

"All I can remember is that night, that last

night, that night. When you leaned down to kiss me and took out your knife. I remember that night. Why did you do that with your knife, Andrei?"

It was no use. She knew someone was close, but she couldn't hear me. Just like Hank could never hear me.

"It's cold." Another voice. A man. "It's so cold."

"I know it's cold, but we got to hold out. We can't be far outside town."

Another male voice, then another:

"We need to get up and walk, or we'll freeze here. I seen it at Camp Douglas during the war. You freeze to death when you stop moving."

"Would you shut up about the war already?"

"We should have stayed with the herd. Why didn't we stay with the herd instead of trying to beat the storm back to town? We could have shot a cow and dragged the guts out and crawled inside. It would have been *warm*."

Five male voices now, some talking at once:

"Too late now to talk about what we should have done."

"We have to get up and walk, or we'll die."

"How far back is the mare the wolves killed, you think? A half mile?"

"I can't tell which way is up or down in the blizzard, much less east or west."

"If we don't know which direction we're

headed, we might be walking away from Dodge."

"The carcass of that mare is frozen stiff by now."

"You think the other horses will come back around?"

"Not a chance with the wolves out there. I can't see them, but I can hear the hungry bastards."

"Do you think the wolves will . . ."

"At Camp Douglas, one man froze to death standing still."

". . . wait until we're dead?"

"They didn't with the mare, did they?"

"I'd like to get just one clean shot at that biggest bastard."

"Reckon we ought to draw lots."

"For what?"

"The man with the short straw kills the others, so we don't commit a mortal sin."

"Then what do you call murdering someone?"

"A mercy."

"What about the man that's left?"

"That's why we draw lots."

"Or maybe we just kill the man with the short straw."

A beat.

"Say what you mean."

"We kill the man what draws the short straw, and we hollow him out—"

"To hell with that. I ain't wearing any of you like a robe."

"That's the stupidest idea you've had yet, Jimpson, and you have been full of stupid ideas from the start, you lumber-headed fool. We start skinning each other and the smell of blood will drive the wolves into a frenzy. We'll all die ugly and painful."

"I can't feel my toes."

"It was just a suggestion. It wasn't like I said we should start eating each other. At least not yet."

"I can't feel *anything*."

"They say it's peaceful, freezing to death. At least, that's what those said at Camp Douglas that nearly froze but were thawed out in time."

"Somebody will find us, right?"

"Sure, by the spring."

"Pretty soon we're not going to be able to . . ."

"Ha! Remember the time Mike McGlue nailed shut all the doors of the privies behind North Front? Now, that was a joke. I can't remember who McGlue was that night. Was it Hoodoo Brown?"

". . . we're not going to be able to . . ."

"No, that was young Tom at the jail."

"We saw some dancin' that night, I'll say."

". . . we won't be able to pull the trigger."

"The camp was on Lake Michigan, and I never felt anything as cold as the snow and ice as it came off that lake. Until now. The Yankees took our clothes away to keep us from escaping, and it weren't right. They starved us."

"When they find us, do you think they'll know who we are?"

"Not after the wolves finish."

"I'll miss old Mike McGlue."

"You know who I'll miss? Captain Drew."

"The whore?"

"The same. Jessie is a wicked girl. I'm sorry I'll never see her again."

"Can't stay awake."

"I'm sorry I called you lumber-headed, Jimpson."

"It don't . . . it don't matter now . . . anyway."

The male voices faded into a murmuring chorus.

A calm, middle-aged male voice called out pleasantly, "What's your game?"

Are you asking me?

"Sit down, son. Name's Charley Morehouse. Now, you don't seem like a lad who is too familiar with the baize tables. There's faro, of course, but that's a game for those who have some practice and skill. There's keno or chuck-a-luck. . . . What? No, I don't remember you. . . . Poker? Don't care for the game. It was popular up in Deadwood, and Hickok was murdered while playing it, shot in the head by a kid named McCall. You're not planning to shoot me, are you? Now, are you?"

"It's so cold. . . . It's so cold."

"Who is there?" In Russian. "Oh, Andy, where have you gone?"

Then all of the voices began talking at once—the buffalo hunters and the gambler and the Russian girl, and then they were joined by a couple of desperates named Texas Hill and Ed Williams, who were killed by the Vigilance Committee, and a carpenter at the Essex Hotel who was somehow shot by the cook. Only the buffalo hunters could hear each other, and the result was a cacophony of ghosts.

It was useless to ask them direct questions. They were all stuck in their own unfinished business, and would be until that business was somehow resolved. The sad part was, they didn't know they were ghosts.

Then the thought occurred to me: Have I become a ghost?

"Ophie, you're not a ghost," a familiar voice said.

You can hear me think?

"You're not exactly thinking or exactly talking, my dear."

Well, Paschal, am I exactly dead?

"You are in between."

Purgatory, then. Are you my Virgil?

"Never. I was too weak."

I'm sorry, Paschal. You were weak and I was . . . desperate.

"Ophie, you're going to have to pull yourself together."

Can I talk to Jonathan now? Jonathan, where are you?

"Don't think about Jonathan."

How I long to talk to Jonathan. You promised, Paschal.

"Please, Ophie. Concentrate."

I never received any message, Paschal. It was all a lie. There is death.

"Of course, death is real. But what comes after is real, too. It's not life, but it's not nothing."

Death is real.

"Ophie, listen to me."

Wait a minute. How can we have this conversation? Ghosts don't answer direct questions.

"I'm not exactly a ghost, Ophie."

There you go using that word "exactly" again.

"I can't explain it any better."

Well, if you're not a ghost, and you're answering direct questions, that means you're a demon. Well, are you?

"Of course not."

A demon answers direct questions, but those answers might be lies.

"That's true."

Unless—unless what? How am I supposed to ask to know the truth?

"I don't know, Ophie."

Yes, you do. You taught me in New Orleans, so long ago, before that morning when you chased me to Jackson Square in the rain. What was the rule? Why can't I think of it now?

"Because you've lost your soul shadow."

Right. Malleus. He took it. He's far below the Arkansas now. That's how the cowboys say it around here—"far below the Arkansas." Like they were describing the underworld.

"Don't die without your aura, Ophie."

I still have my soul.

"But not your soul's complement. You're just half yourself."

This is confusing, Paschal.

"You have a choice to make."

Perhaps I should just go ahead and cross over.

"No."

I hate you.

"I know."

Then why should I listen to you?

"Because right now, I'm the only friend you've got."

Why should you even care?

"Let's just say, you're my unfinished business."

Now, that sounds ghostly.

"You've got work to do, Ophie."

What work?

"First you have to find your aura."

But how?

"That is for you to work out."

And then?

"Your life will have purpose, if you choose it."

What kind of purpose?

"You have a gift, Ophie. You've always had the gift."

But why can I hear them now?

"You've had the intense shock required to break the grip your senses had on illusory reality. You've reconnected with your childhood gift. And you could use this gift to help people, instead of taking out your frustration over Jonathan on the gullible and the greedy."

I don't think that's what I've been doing, exactly.

"There's proof you're not dead yet. You're lying, and the dead don't lie."

It's kind of peaceful here. What if I choose not to go back?

"Then you become just another ghost of Boot Hill."

I've been here too long. I'm surely dead.

"You have to choose."

But I don't have enough information. If you're a demon, you might be lying to me, or you might not be. This would not be the first time you've led me down the path to damnation.

"Choose, Ophie."

If I pass over now, will I see Jonathan?

No response.

"In a moment, you're going to see a light. It's going to be dim at first, and then it will grow stronger. In that light, you're going to see people—relatives and friends, mostly—whom you have not seen in a long time. You might see other beings, too—not human beings, but entities that perhaps you've doubted these many long years."

You're talking in riddles, Paschal. Be clear.

"The light will be warm and loving and you're going to want to go toward it."

And Jonathan will be there?

"No."

Why not?

Off in the distance, where there was no distance, a glow appeared. It was shimmering white and came gradually closer. It was a little like the reflection of the full moon when you see it rippling on the surface of the Mississippi, a little like seeing daylight at the end of a long train tunnel, and a lot like looking up at the sky from the bottom of a well. But all at once.

Is my Tanté Marie there?

"No."

There were figures moving in the light.

All right, Paschal. I've decided.

"Don't tell me. I don't have the power. Tell *her.*"

Stepping out of the light was a shimmering figure in white, the most beautiful woman— and yet not a woman—I've ever seen. The angel was smiling and she held out her hands to me. The love I felt coming from her overwhelmed me. I felt clean, as if I'd never had a trouble in the world, as if I had been forgiven for every wrong thing I'd ever done. I wanted to throw myself into those loving arms and leave everything behind.

Then, behind me, I heard a pitiful voice calling softly, "Who is there? Andrei?"

Take her, too. Please.

We cannot.

"Look, I have the pearly button I tore from your pocket. Let me sew it back on for you. I'm sorry I ruined your favorite shirt."

She's not ready.

That doesn't seem fair.

It's not about fairness.

It doesn't seem just.

It is not for us to decide.

Isn't there any justice on the other side?

There is only perfect truth and perfect peace.

No fairness or justice?

Justice is up to the living.

"Andy! Why have you left me?" the Russian girl cried out once more.

Choose.

I'm not ready. There are things left undone.

25

Suddenly shot back into my body, I vibrated with only one thought: *to breathe.* My lungs burned for air and my brain felt as if it would burst, and I felt the burlap sack being jerked up and out of the grave. Then there was the sound of a blade cutting the rope and slitting the sack, and the night air brushed my cheeks.

A dark figure stood over me, knife in hand.

I pleaded with wide eyes.

Jack Calder threw the knife into the ground and knelt. He placed one hand behind my head, while he hooked a finger in my mouth and dislodged a clump of dirt and sand.

"Breathe," he said. "Breathe!"

Then he pushed me forward and slapped me between the shoulder blades so hard that I thought my ribs would break. Still, I could not force air into my lungs. Blotches of red and black and brown stained my vision.

"Damn it," Calder said. "I will not lose you."

He pulled me back, put his left arm beneath me, took a great gulp of air, and then put his mouth on mine. As he forced his breath into me, I could feel his chin stubble bruising my jaw, smell the sweat that stained his collar, and taste the coffee and cigar he'd had not long before.

Then my lungs fluttered and trembled. When his lips released mine, I greedily sucked in air, but I could not seem to get enough. I gasped and coughed and shook for more as Calder held my shoulders.

"Slow down," he said. "You can't drink in the whole night sky at once."

Then he picked me up and carried me down from Boot Hill into town, along North Front, where the cowboys and gamblers and whores gave way for us, and to the door of City Drug. He kicked the door so hard that it splintered the bottom hinges.

"Who the hell is breaking down my door?" Doc McCarty called from the back room.

"We need you, Doc."

Calder carried me into the room and put me down on the same table that Shadrach had died on. Doc emerged from the back, pulling up his suspenders and holding a coal oil lamp.

"Tell me, quick."

Doc was leaning down and was lifting each

of my eyelids with his thumb while shining the lamplight in my eyes.

"That damn fool Murdock threw her in the open grave on Boot Hill."

"Just threw her in?"

"And buried her."

"How long was she under?"

"Couldn't have been very long," Calder said. "A few minutes, maybe."

No, I tried to say. It was much longer than a few minutes. All night, it seemed. But Doc was now looking down my throat and examining my nose and ears.

"I met Murdock and two new friends on Tin Pot Alley, and one of them had a shovel slung over his shoulder," Calder said. "I had seen Miss Wylde earlier at the Saratoga. But before I knew it, she had slipped out. I had a bad feeling something like this was going to happen, Doc."

"And you just knew what Murdock had done?"

"He told me after I beat him with the shovel."

"How bad did you hurt him?"

"Pay attention to the patient in front of you, Doc."

McCarty frowned, but he leaned over and spoke in my face.

"Do you know your name, dear?"

I didn't answer right away.

After a few minutes, he asked again.

"Can you tell me your name?"

"Want me to spell it, too? It has a *Y* in there."

Up like thunder, my mind was back.

"She's all right."

"How do you know I'm all right? You haven't looked at me for thirty seconds. There could be all sorts of things wrong with me from being at the bottom of a grave. Just the grave air alone might have given me something."

"You have some dirt packed in your nose and ears," McCarty said. "That's all. Your eyes react to light well, nothing appears broken, and your mind is obviously intact. Your coastal defenses are manned and ready, as usual."

I paused.

"Was it awful?" McCarty asked.

"Doc," I said, "I was scared witless."

"It was a cruel thing to do," McCarty said. "And likely fatal, if Jack Calder hadn't been watching out for you."

"Why would you do that?" I asked.

"Anybody would have dug you out."

"No," I said. "I mean, watch out for me."

Calder shrugged.

"I don't know, either," I said.

McCarty had pulled on his shirt now, and he was gathering up some things in a little satchel.

"Where's Murdock?"

"Still on the alley off Chestnut, I reckon."

"Then I guess I'd better go have a look," McCarty said. "Jack, the old days of the Vigilance Committee are over. You can't just go around beating confessions out of people. You'll wind up with a murder charge yourself."

"Are you saying I should have let her die?"

"I'm rather glad you didn't," McCarty said, and winked at me.

"Doc," I said.

"Yes?"

"It was fearful, at first. Voices. But there was something else. Something peaceful. It wasn't Summerland. But it was . . . something good. Angelic, even. A part of me was sad to come back."

McCarty thought for a moment.

"If I were of a judgmental nature," he said, "I might say that sounds like humbug to me—childish, as you told me not long ago. Or, if I were strictly a man of science, I might say that during suffocation one blacks out and is prone to fantasies. But I am just a man."

"Then what do you say as just a man, Doc?"

"That the wise among us know where the limits of their wisdom stop," he said. "It seems you have found yours. Welcome back to the race of human animals, Miss Wylde."

I didn't know what to say.

"A long, hot bath—that's what I recommend," McCarty said. Then he frowned as he slid past the broken door. "Did you have to kick it in, Jack? You know where the key is."

"I was in a hurry," Calder said.

"Well, you're going to have to pay to get it fixed."

McCarty left.

"Let's find you a bath," Calder said.

"Where?" I asked. "It must be three o'clock in the morning. The Dodge House has long since closed the bathing rooms."

"You can get a bath twenty-four hours a day here during cattle drive season," Calder said. "There are two or three bathhouses down on South Front, and two of them are in tents."

"It doesn't sound very private."

"It is, if you're willing to pay," Calder said. "I'll come with you."

"I think not."

"I meant that I would stand guard outside."

Calder propped the door of the City Drug back in its frame and locked it with a key he took from the nearest rain barrel. He shoved on the door, and it only gave a little toward the bottom. He pronounced it good enough for now.

We walked across the tracks to South Front, where we found a big canvas concern that was all lit up from the inside. There were plenty of tubs inside and water being heated over fires, and a dozen cowboys or so were sitting in tubs in the main part, soaking off the trail dust. Most were smoking cigars or leisurely sipping whiskey. A few of them had girls in little or no clothing helping to scrub.

For three bucks, we got a private tub in the back, with a canvas partition. It didn't take long to fill the tub with hot water, and Calder grabbed a stool and sat outside while I undressed.

"If you slide those clothes out under the tarp," Calder said, "we can get them washed."

"Now?"

"Where you have hot water, you have a laundry," he said. "They won't be dry until morning, but we can find something for you to wear back to the Dodge House."

I came to the tarp and passed my filthy clothes beneath it. I was aware that the lamp near the tub was throwing my shadow on the canvas. I didn't mean to be provocative; I was just bone-tired. I nodded toward modesty, however, by keeping my arms folded and my legs together.

I slid into the tub. It felt so good that I closed my eyes and emitted a slight moan.

"You want a cigar?" Calder asked.

"No, thanks," I said. "And you've apparently already had one tonight."

"How did you—"

"I tasted it."

"I like to smoke in the evenings," he said. "It's relaxing."

"It's a filthy habit," I said.

But it didn't seem so filthy when I imagined Calder smoking.

"It is somewhat less filthy," he said, "compared to many other vices."

"True," I said, scrubbing my left arm.

"Mrs. Wylde," Calder said. "May I ask—"

"You have earned the right to call me Ophelia, I think."

"Ophelia," he said, "what you told Doc about the angel or whatever . . ."

"Yes?"

"Is that true?"

"It wasn't part of my act, if that's what you're getting at," I said.

"That's not it," he said. "I was curious as to whether any revelations accompanied the angelic visitation."

There was something, wasn't there? I tried to remember.

"I'm not sure," I said. "No, wait. There were a lot of voices. There was a girl, speaking Russian."

"Russian?"

"Yes, the dead girl. She talked about her throat being cut. There were also a gambler and buffalo hunters. They talked about a cyprian called Captain Drew. Was there ever such a woman by that name here?"

"There was, years ago," Calder said. "Jessie Drew. They called her 'Captain Drew' because she bossed all the other whores around. She moved on a couple of years ago. Went to New Mexico, I think."

I vigorously used a brush to dislodge the dirt from my fingernails.

"Is there anybody who speaks Russian in Kansas?"

"There are the Russian Mennonites up the Santa Fe tracks around Newton," Calder said. "A town called Alexanderwohl. Thousands of them came over three years ago from the Crimea, to avoid military service in the czar's army. They are pacifists, apparently, and wheat farmers."

"But why Kansas?"

"The climate's about the same as the Crimea, and the Santa Fe sold them thousands of acres to grow their wheat. Nobody gave them a chance in hell of making it, but they have this hard winter strain they brought with them, something called Turkey Red, which seems to be working."

"But we're a long way from Newton, right?"

"Two hundred miles, give or take. But that's only five hours by train."

"Strange how distance is relative, now," I said. "Five hours back east to Newton. But if you walk north or south out of Dodge, you're what—only five miles outside of town in five hours?"

"Or twenty miles on horseback," Calder said. "No, the railroad means money. Dodge City wouldn't be going like hot peanuts if it wasn't for the railroad. Cattle, hides . . ."

I thought of the wagon caravan of hides.

"What do they do with all those hides, anyway?"

"They cut them up to make belts to drive machinery back East. Whether it's steam power or water power, the power has to be transmitted to the pulleys somehow, and buffalo hide is cheap and wears well. Also, the bones can be ground into fertilizer."

"So the buffalo are being turned into the very things that hasten their demise—fertilizer for farmland and pulleys to drive machinery that produces everything from guns to barbed wire."

"How is that different than the Comanche using buffalo meat for food and the hide for their lodges and the tails for fly swatters?"

"One is a matter of need," I said. "The other is just an example of greed."

"I have a coat with buttons made of buffalo bone," Calder said. "Does that make me needy or greedy?"

Something stirred in my memory. "What?" I asked.

"I said, I have a coat—"

"Buttons," I said. "The dead girl who spoke Russian was talking about a button she had torn from the shirt of the man who killed her. And when I saw her ghost, she was clutching something tight in her right hand."

"A button?"

"It must be," I said. "Do you know if Doc McCarty examined the girl before she was buried?"

"There was no reason to," Calder said. "She was quite dead."

"But did anybody open her hand?"

"She was stiff as a board. The undertaker didn't want her, because there was no money in it, so we took up a collection for lumber and built a rough coffin and placed her in it. Nobody thought to force open her hand."

I sat up in the tub.

"Jack," I said. "We've got to dig her up."

Calder protested that exhumation was a legal process and required a court order. He also rattled off some stuff from Blackstone saying that common law viewed the final resting place of a human being as sacred, and that disturbing those remains was a serious offense. Only a family member could petition for exhumation, he said, or the church, if the burial was in consecrated ground. He said he didn't think there was anything consecrated about Boot Hill, though.

"You dug me up," I said.

"You weren't dead."

"Who can order an exhumation, then?"

"Judge Grout, but I'm not sure he would grant the petition based on your visit to the other world," Calder said. "Grout may be soft about his poor dead boy, but he would be pretty hardheaded about this. There would have to be compelling evidence, and we don't have it. The only other person who can order it would be the coroner, in the course of a police investigation."

"Who's the coroner?"

"Doc Galland," Calder said. "But that old Prussian is unlikely to be sympathetic to our request, unless we could deliver it in High German. But he's not even in town this weekend—he took the train east to Kansas City to visit an old friend."

"Who's the assistant coroner?"

"Doc McCarty."

26

We were back at Boot Hill at dawn, standing in the chill air with Doc McCarty and that walrus of a marshal, Larry Deger, who clasped a mug of coffee in his hands and seemed unwilling to share. We were watching as Diamond Jim Murdock and his two miscreant friends took shovelfuls of earth from the grave of the murdered girl and added it to a growing pile alongside. Calder had fetched the trio from the jail and forced them to help, as a fitting— if partial—punishment for what they had done to me the night before.

Murdock had a knot on his forehead the size of a baseball, from where Calder had clobbered him with the shovel handle, and his right eye was swollen shut.

None of the three would look at me while they dug.

My own clothes weren't yet dry from the laundry, so Calder had borrowed some clothes from Tom the Jailer. He was skinny enough, but I had to roll up the sleeves of the flannel shirt and pin the cuffs of the Levi's.

"Can we rest now?" Murdock asked, leaning on the shovel handle and looking up at us.

"Did I tell you to stop digging?" Calder asked.

"I'm really tired," Murdock whined. "My head is throbbing from where you poleaxed me last night. I think I'm going to be sick."

"Your head would have throbbed from the whiskey anyway," McCarty said.

"I don't know why I drink," Murdock said. "It makes me into somebody else and I do things I'm ashamed of."

"You'll have a lot of time in jail to think about what you did," Calder said. "But right now, keep digging."

Murdock made a face and scooped another shovelful of dirt.

"We had better find something in that hole, Calder," Deger said, then slurped his coffee. "If you don't, Doc Galland is going to have your testicles pickled and put in one of those specimen jars and make a present of them to Judge Grout."

"Don't double down yet, Larry," Calder said.

Then a shovel swung by one of the miscreants struck wood.

"It am the coffin."

"Okay, work toward the edges now."

In a few minutes, the dirt had been cleared

away from the edges of the coffin. The grave wasn't the proverbial six feet, but it was a good four or five, and it took a few minutes of struggle for the inmates to work a pair of ropes beneath the coffin. Then they scrambled out of the grave, and each took an end of rope. Calder took the remaining end, and on his count, they began to haul the coffin to the surface.

Soon, the men had the wooden box out and placed beside the grave, and then they began to work on the lid with crowbars and claw hammers. The nails made a frightening screeching sound as they were drawn from the wood. Then the lid was loose, and Calder looked over at Doc.

"You might want to step away now," McCarty suggested.

"No," I said. "I want to see what I would have looked like if Calder hadn't gotten to me in time."

"Suit yourself," McCarty said, and produced a jar of camphor from his pocket. He opened the bottle and allowed Calder and Deger to dip their kerchiefs in it. Then he tore his handkerchief in two, for us both to use.

"All right," McCarty said. "Open her up."

Calder swung the lid off.

We all held the cloths to our noses and mouths, but the stench of decay was overpowering, at once repellent and oddly sweet. All of the miscreants stumbled back many steps, and Murdock fell on his knees and began to retch.

"Go farther down the hill for that," Calder called.

The girl was on her back, her hands crossed over her chest, and her hair spread over her shoulders. Her eyes were closed but sunken. Her skin was a greenish gray. Her black lips had drawn back to reveal her white teeth, which gave the impression that she was smiling without mirth.

The slit beneath her chin still gaped, and it was black with crusted blood.

"*Andrei!*" I heard. "*Is that you? Where are you?*"

Calder knelt down and reached for her left hand.

"The other one," I said.

He stopped.

"You want me to do that, Jack?" McCarty asked. "I'm the acting coroner."

"I can do it, Doc," he said.

But his face showed some doubt.

He reached over again and picked up the girl's right wrist. Having long since passed rigor mortis, her hand unclenched as he lifted it. A bit of something fell from the dead fingers. Calder retrieved the object from the coffin and held it up.

It was a mother-of-pearl button sewn to a ragged patch of black cloth.

"I'll be damned," Deger said.

"I'd say that looks like a button from Andrew

Vanderslice's favorite shirt," Calder said. "What do you think, Doc?"

"I think you need a warrant," McCarty said.

"I already have a warrant for Vanderslice," Calder said. "A federal writ for selling whiskey to the Comanches, and I aim to serve it."

"Shouldn't you wait until Judge Grout can issue one tomorrow morning?"

"That's going to give Vanderslice another twenty-four hours ahead of me," Calder said. "The murder charge can be filed after I drag him back."

Calder handed the button and cloth to McCarty for safekeeping.

"Marshal, you might want to contact the Russian Mennonite community, up near Newton, and see if any of their girls are missing. I expect them to say yes."

"What makes you think that?" Deger asked.

"Call it a hunch," Calder said as he rested the lid back on the coffin.

"Like the button?"

"I told you, Doc had a confidential witness for that, somebody who wouldn't come forward if his name was used," Calder said. Then he stood and used the camphor handkerchief on his hands. "All right, boys. Seal her up and get her back into the ground."

"Wait," I said.

"For what?" Calder asked.

"We should say something."

"She's right," McCarty said.

"Go ahead," Calder said to me.

"I'm no preacher."

"You're the closest thing we've got," McCarty said.

"All right."

I told the men to doff their hats, although Calder wasn't wearing a hat, as usual. Then I cleared my throat and bowed my head.

"I wish you could hear me," I said. "Because if you could, I'd tell you that you aren't forgotten, that even if we don't know your name, there are good people here who care about what happened to you. We're going to try to help you find some rest."

27

"I'm going with you," I said.

"You can't. You've got the hearing in front of Judge Grout tomorrow," Calder said, taking some kind of rifle down from an antelope-horned rack on the wall. We were in his quarters, behind the law offices of Frazier and Hunnicutt, across from the courthouse. The entire living space was one room, really just a shack added to the back of the law office. It was filled with the usual kinds of trash that bachelors tend to accumulate: papers, dirty clothes, dishes that needed washing. There was a potbelly stove in one corner and a rope bed opposite.

"If you don't show up," Calder said, "Grout is going to issue a warrant for your arrest and somebody like me is going to track you down and send you to Labette County to stand trial as Kate Bender."

"Potete can fix that."

"You don't understand," Calder said. "I might be gone for two or three weeks, and Potete can't fix anything if you're not there."

I leaned against the wall and crossed my arms. There wasn't room to sit, because every flat surface was piled with something—legal documents, law books, dirty plates. Even the chairs had bundles of the *Times* and other newspapers on them.

"How do you live like this?"

"Sorry, I didn't know I was going to have guests."

"Where are your books?"

"The law books are in the corner."

"No, I mean literature."

"I read newspapers."

"But not Twain or Dickens."

"I only read factual material."

"There's more fiction in just one edition of the *Kansas City Times* than in all of Thackeray," I said, aiming at sounding droll but grazing boorish, instead. "Look at this mess! You can hardly walk from room to room."

"I know where everything is."

"Every man says that," I said. "You're going to burn this place down, come winter, when you light that stove. A single spark could set the whole mess on fire."

"Worry about your own problems, Professor Wylde."

"I am, and that's why I demand to come with you."

"You're not in a position to demand anything."

He began gathering cartridge boxes.

"Look, Jack," I said. "There's something I have to get back from the creature Vanderslice works for, this Malleus. He stole it from me, and if I don't get it back, then none of these other things matter."

"Your aura," Calder said. "You already told me that at the drugstore."

"Then why don't you believe me?"

"It sounds crazy."

I made an incredulous sound in my throat. "How much more proof do you need that this stuff is real?" I asked. "What about the button? I couldn't have just made that up."

"That's different," Calder said. "That came to you in a vision or something. But this thing about your aura . . . I've never heard anything like that before. If everybody has an aura, then why have I never seen one?"

"Because you haven't looked," I said. "It takes some practice."

"What color is mine, then?"

"Green," I said.

"That's not my favorite color."

"I know—your favorite color is blue."

He gave me an odd look.

"I guessed that, because of your shirts. You're

always wearing a blue shirt under that vest. But auras don't work like that. It's not based on your favorite color. It has to do with your mood and personality."

"Even if that's true," he said, "there's no reason you should go with me. It's too dangerous. And with you along—well, I'd always be looking out for you and not concentrating on bringing in Vanderslice."

"I can take care of myself. I have, for a long time."

"Not like this," he said. "Below the Arkansas is no man's land. There's nobody to ask for help when you get in trouble, and the only thing you can count on is trouble."

"All the more reason for me to go with you."

He picked up the rifle and offered it, butt-first.

"Tell me whether this is loaded or not," he said.

"I don't like guns."

"Take it," he said, and shoved it in my hands. I hated the feel of it.

"Gun help is the only kind of help I need," he said. "And you can't even tell me if it's loaded or not, much less how to use the damned thing."

He took the rifle from me.

"I can be useful in other ways," I suggested.

"Like what?"

"I'm smart," I said. "And I knew the girl had that button in her hand. There could be other things that would come to me from the dead. And the dead always tell the truth, Jack."

He began shoving cartridges into the bottom of the rifle.

"I know you don't understand about the aura," I said. "But if I don't get it back, I'm never going to be myself."

"You seem fine to me."

"I won't be for long," I said. "Without my aura, I'll turn into somebody else. It'll happen so gradual that nobody will notice the change, at least not at first. But it's already started. Remember the mezcal binge? When you met me, I was at McCarty's seeking a cure for a hangover. That's not me, Jack. And when I channeled Katie Bender? I don't know if that was her or not, but it was *something* evil. These things won't stop until I have my aura back."

He stopped loading the gun. "What happens if you die without it?"

"I don't know, Jack. I'm scared."

He sighed and then muttered beneath his breath.

"Can you ride?"

28

I had grown up with Tennessee walking horses, the kind of mount that plantation owners would survey their acres from. Such horses were known for their gentle ways and easy ride. What I needed was something fast and tough. So, at Bell Livery on Third, south of the deadline, I chose an Arabian mare named Fatima and a Texas saddle—although Bell first tried to sell me a sidesaddle. I said to have both horse and tack ready in half an hour, and then I went to the Dodge House. There I packed what little I owned into the valise, including the take from the performances at the opera house—just over five hundred dollars and change. It would be just enough to settle up at the Dodge House, buy the horse and saddle, and a few incidentals. I had picked up my regular clothes at the laundry, and I left the flannel and denim borrowed from Tom the Jailer on the bed.

There was only one thing left to do.

I opened the window over Front Street.

The problem with ravens and other corvids is that once they imprint on a person, it's for life. If given to another owner, they become deeply melancholic and often will themselves dead. I had raised Eddie since he was just a baby. If I left him for someone else to take care of, even somebody as kind as Doc McCarty, odds were that Eddie would soon become miserable and would eventually die. So there was only one thing to do.

I opened the cage and reached my hand in. Eddie rubbed his beak against my fingers, the membrane over his eyes half closing in contentment. Then I took him out of the cage and held him for a moment on my forearm, stroking his gleaming blue-black feathers.

"I'm sorry, Eddie," I said. "My hand is played out and I'm about to jump off the edge of the world for God knows where. I don't expect to come back, considering the amount of weaponry Calder was preparing, and from the tone of his voice. But if I don't go, I'm never going to get my aura back. It's better to die trying than to just sit and waste away into somebody else, don't you think?"

He cocked his head.

"I know. It's all my fault. I'm so sorry."

I started to cry.

"At least this way, you'll have a chance," I said. "Ravens are smart, and you're the smartest of them all. Why, if you could learn the things I taught you, you will do just fine on your own. But you'll have to look out for hawks and eagles, and probably hang around town so you can eat scraps the restaurants throw out their back doors. I recommend Tin Pot Alley, since there always seems to be fresh slop there."

I wiped my eyes with the back of my free hand.

"And who knows?" I told him. "Maybe I will come back, and you'll still be here in Dodge, and you'll find me and we'll be like we always were—inseparable. What do you think, baby? We'll meet again, right?"

"'Nevermore.'"

Now I was truly bawling.

I carried him to the open window.

"Go on," I said.

He didn't budge.

"Take off," I said. "You're free."

He swiveled his head to look at me with first one eye, and then the other.

"Fly, damn it!"

I shoved my arm out the window and shook it, and Eddie squawked and snarled and dug his claws into my arm, trying to hang on. Then I shook harder, and Eddie flew off. He swung out low over North Front, flapped over the train depot, and then turned sharply, coming back to the hotel.

I slammed the window shut.

29

Calder met me at the livery. He was riding a big bay. The enormous rifle in a scabbard was tied to the saddle, and the ridiculously large revolver was set on his hip. He was also wearing a hat, a no-nonsense tan felt hat with a wide brim.

"Good horse," he said when I brought out the Arabian.

"My father knew horses," I said. "He passed some of that down to me."

Calder had brought an extra tarp and bedroll, which I tied behind my saddle.

"I brought you something," Calder said, reaching behind to take something from back of the saddle. Then he held out a woman's hat, a lady's black riding hat, with a high crown and narrow brim. There were black ribbons trailing down the back.

I took it reluctantly.

"I know it's not a gentleman's hat, which you

would prefer," he said. "But you need a hat, and
with this one, you can tie the ribbons beneath
your chin if there's a wind, and at least it has
some brim to protect you from the sun. It
belongs . . . Well, it used to belong to somebody
I know, but they have no use for it anymore."

"I'm not her, Jack."

"I know," he said quickly, and rubbed his jaw,
as if the words ached in his mouth. "It's just a
hat. Wear it or not."

He nudged the bay forward.

I put on the hat and followed.

We rode down dusty Locust Street, past the
sleepy saloons and the tired brothels, where the
inhabitants were loitering in doorways with
cups of coffee or glasses of whiskey in their
hands, cigarettes dangling from their lips. They
watched us pass without saying a word or giving
a wave of greeting. As we approached Bridge
Street, the bell at the Union Church on Gospel
Ridge began to ring. I knew it was because a
preacher had been sent down the tracks from
Emporia or Newton or Topeka to hold services.
But in my bones, it felt like the bell was tolling
for me and for Calder.

Then we turned south on Bridge Street, and
just south of town we had to pay a toll of a
dollar apiece at the big wooden bridge across
the Arkansas River. We passed a cottonwood
tree and Calder told me to take a good look at
it, because it would be the last tree for a good,
long while.

At points not far south of Dodge, we had our pick of trails that veered off, including the Western Trail, the Adobe Walls Trail, and the Jones and Plummer Trail, which led to Fort Elliott. All of these trails had been opened up in 1875 because the last free bands of Comanche and Kiowa had been rounded up and put on reservations near Fort Sill, deep in Indian Territory.

Thus began three days of hard travel over hard country.

After we left the Arkansas River Valley, the land flattened and dried out, but it wasn't so bad because we met a few herds coming north. We could parlay with the cowboys who traveled with them, and sometimes spared a few minutes for coffee or beans at the chuck wagons that preceded the herds. The weather was pleasant enough, not too hot and not too cold. Once or twice, we were soaked by a sudden shower.

Then we entered No Man's Land, a narrow strip of land between Texas and Kansas that had been set aside for the Indians to hunt buffalo, but which had been opened up after the Indians were imprisoned on the reservation. The deeper we went in No Man's Land, the lonelier we became. Calder said we were gaining ground on the supply caravan. He could tell because of the freshness of the dung left by the oxen.

On the afternoon of the third day, we entered a rolling plain, and Calder said we had crossed over into Texas. Close to sundown, we came upon a little cabin next to a creek. Calder expressed surprise.

"Don't remember this," he said.

"You've been this way before," I said.

"Not in years," he said. "Last time I was here, all of this was controlled by the Kiowa and Comanche. Anybody who put down stakes here would be asking to be burned out, and worse. I guess times have changed. Let's see what the occupants have seen in the past couple of days. Act friendly and keep your hands out where the folks in the cabin can see them, so they know you aren't hiding a gun."

We rode up to within thirty yards of the cabin and stopped.

"Aren't you going to say something?" I asked.

"Nope," Calder said. "They're looking us over to decide if they want to invite us in or not."

So we sat there, and the rest gave me time to study the sky beyond the cabin. There was a wicked-looking line of clouds in the southwest, their flat bottoms dark with rain, and their tops ascending the sky like castle walls. A gentle wind was preceding the storm, but no rain yet.

After another minute or so, the cabin door swung open on leather hinges. A young man stood in the doorway, holding a shotgun in both hands. His suspenders were down and his feet were bare, as if he had just rolled out of bed.

"Looking for trouble?" the man asked.

"Not particularly," Calder said.

"Are you with them?"

"Mister," Calder said, "we're with nobody but ourselves. Sorry to bother you. We'll be on our way."

Calder tugged the brim of his hat and turned his horse, and I followed.

"Wait!" the man called.

"Is there something we can do for you?" Calder asked over his shoulder.

"You can tell me if I've gone crazy or not," he said. "Yesterday the supply train bound for Fort Elliott came by here. They crossed the creek at the rocky ford yonder."

"Was a whiskey trader by the name of Vanderslice with them?"

"There was a whiskey trader, but I don't know his name."

"Tall? Good-looking?" I asked.

"He was vain, if that's what you mean."

We turned back and walked our horses to within a few yards of the cabin.

"What you got that scattergun loaded with?" Calder asked.

"Dimes. A dollar of silver in each barrel."

"What has you so rattled?" Calder asked.

"Mister, I saw a man turn into a wolf yesterday."

"That a fact?" Calder asked.

"Saw a man turn into a wolf and rip the stuffing out of my brother like he was just a rag doll, right here in front of the cabin. So I figure I'm either going crazy or there is something powerful evil on the loose. Either way, it don't sit easy with me."

"You're not crazy," I said, dismounting. "My name is Ophelia Wylde, and this is my partner, Jack Calder. I talk to the dead, and Jack's a bounty hunter. We're on the trail of this evil thing you saw yesterday. Do you mind if we come in and talk?"

The man invited us in, but kept the shotgun across his lap as he sat at a table with his back to the wall. He said his name was Pollux Adams and that he was twenty-five years old and that he had been a cowboy driving herds from the panhandle over to the Western Trail. He said he liked this little patch of land along Kiowa Creek enough that he came back with his brother, Castor, and filed a claim, becoming the first white settler in probably fifty miles. That had been a year ago. And apart from the occasional Indian scare, things had gone right well—until yesterday.

The wagon caravan bossed by Malleus had always made him uneasy, he said, but it had never given him any trouble. The train had a dozen or so rangy bullwhackers who seemed more animal than human, but that wasn't unusual for bullwhackers, because they were a rough sort. But these bullwhackers, he said, were rougher than usual, and he never heard them speak—just snarl and snap at one another. Yesterday afternoon the Malleus train rattled over the ford as usual, but one of the whackers seemed particularly aggressive. Castor and Pollux Adams were cooking up some supper on the little stove inside the cabin, just jackrabbit stew and corn bread, and the whacker came right into the cabin and lunged for the pot. He burned himself, of course, spilled the stew all over the floor, and scrambled like a wounded animal on all fours as he slunk away. Castor gave him a swift kick in the ribs for his trouble, and the man yelped and snapped at him before running out the door.

"It was the damndest thing I ever saw," Pollux Adams said. "The man behaved just like an animal. Castor and me laughed about it, and then we cleaned up the mess on the floor, and salvaged what jackrabbit meat we could, and started another batch. We ate supper, and had a smoke, and sat outside while it grew dark."

A blast of wind hit the cabin and rattled the shutters as Pollux told us his tale. The cabin door was open, as were the shutters on the windows, and the air and sky had turned an odd green hue.

"I don't like the color of outside," Calder said.

"What happened next?" I asked, ignoring him.

"It was twilight when the whacker came back," Pollux said in a voice so low we had to listen hard to catch every word. "He had stayed hidden down by the creek while the train had moved on. He walked up like a man, but by the time he got to the night shadow of the cabin, he was a wolf—a big gray one with yellow eyes."

"What did you do?" I asked.

"We both were so surprised, we didn't do anything for a moment—like that feeling you get in dreams when you're scared but can't move," Pollux said. "But we came out of it pretty quick when we realized the wolf was coming at us. Both Castor and me are in the habit of keeping our pieces in our belts, because you never know out here when you're going to need them right quick, and we both drew down on the rangy beast and fired. I can't conceive of how we missed, but apparently we did. The wolf didn't even slow down. When he was about six feet out, he jumped and landed square on Castor's chest and tore open his throat like he was bringing down a calf."

There was a flash of lightning outside, followed a split second later by thunder, which shook dust from the rafters. Then came the patter of rain on the shake roof.

"Ophelia, we need to get the horses under that pole and thatched stable out back," Calder said.

"Jack, I need to hear the rest of this story."

"All right," Calder said, heading for the door. "I reckon I'll take care of the horses."

"What happened next, Pollux?"

"I placed the barrel of my pistol against the wolf's head and blew his brains out, and he rolled over dead on the spot. But it was too late for Castor. His throat had been ripped out and his chest mauled right bad. It looked like the wolf was trying to break right through his ribs to his heart."

Pollux hung his head nearly to his knees and wept.

"I buried Castor out back," he said. "But something came and dug him up and carried his body away."

I put a hand on his shoulder. "Did the wolf you shot turn back into a man?"

"Nope," Pollux said. "I dragged the carcass down by the river and burned it up. But the odd thing was, I found this in the ashes when it was all done."

He reached into his pocket and produced what looked like a marble—brown and swirled-red glass.

"Feel it," he said. He placed it in my palm.

It was as heavy as lead, and I gasped as pain like fire shot up my arm and into my chest. I dropped it on the floor, where it didn't bounce and stayed put as if glued.

"Strange, ain't it?"

"It is wicked strange," I said. "Pollux, do you know where the whiskey trader goes when he leaves the train?"

"Yeah. He and Malleus both hole up—"

Then there was an odd sound outside, as if

a locomotive trailing a thousand cars was bearing down on us. Calder burst in the door and told us to get to the root cellar.

"What's wrong?" I asked.

"Cyclone."

"Cellar's around back," Pollux said. "It ain't deep, but it will do."

On the way around back, Calder stopped long enough at the thatched stable to untie the horses and slap them on the flank to get them moving toward the creek. They were still saddled, as all he'd had time for was to loosen the cinch straps.

Calder grabbed my hand and pulled me toward the cellar door.

Then I looked to the southwest and gasped.

A cyclone was snaking across the field, not three hundred yards from where we stood. It was dark and sinewy and was chewing up dirt and grass, and it was murmuring a dead language.

Calder shoved me down into the cellar and stood there by the open door, calling for Pollux Adams. But instead of running for cover, Pollux stood his ground.

"Where's the hideout?" I shouted.

He turned and said something, but I couldn't hear him.

"What?"

Now he was walking toward the cyclone, his shotgun at the ready.

"Ciudad Perdida!"

Then he planted his feet and shouldered the

gun. But before he could fire, the cyclone picked him up and tossed him in the air like a rag doll. There was a bright tongue of flame from both barrels of the gun, and I could see the glittering dimes spread against the darkening sky.

Calder pulled me down into the cellar and pressed me to the ground while the storm raged above us. Then we heard a terrible creaking and snapping of wood. The entire cabin was lifted away and torn apart, so much lumber being sucked into the whirling sky above us.

30

Calder handed me my hat, which he found on the ground near where the cabin had stood just minutes before. The sky had turned a normal color for evening, a pale blue, and Venus shone brightly in the west, the storm having passed.

"Are you all right?" Calder asked.

"Relatively speaking," I said. "Odd the storm didn't take the hat."

"Everything about what just happened was odd."

"Poor Pollux!"

"At least he went out fighting—although you're going to need something more than a scattergun to go up against a cyclone."

"It wasn't an ordinary kind of storm," I said. "Malleus was behind it, I could feel him in the wind. If he can summon forces like that . . ."

"Want to turn back?"

"No," I said. "Do you know this place, *Ciudad Perdida*?"

It meant "Lost City."

"I've heard of it," Calder said. "Some call it 'Buried City.'"

"What is it?"

"Ruins," he said, brushing the mud from his own hat and trying to restore some shape. He had jammed it beneath him in the cellar. "Maybe twenty miles west along the creek. They're very old."

"Spanish, then?" I asked. "The conquistadors?"

"Older than that," Calder said. "The Spanish found it three hundred years ago, and it was already very old then. It stretches for miles along the creek, an entire city carved out beneath the rocky bluffs along the creek. Maybe one of the Lost Tribes of Israel built it."

"Or some kind of Indian civilization we don't know about yet."

Calder looked sour.

"All Indians know how to do is kill," he said. "If there were Indians here before the Comanche, then they were killers, too. It's their way."

I began to object, but his face told me I should let it drop.

"We'd better round up the horses," Calder said. "We'll find them in the low ground, down by the creek."

* * *

We found the horses. Calder suggested we make camp, because it was full night and we didn't want to be stumbling around in the dark. I agreed, but was uneasy about sleeping near the open cellar, where the cabin had been. We walked the horses onto the plain, a few hundred yards to the west, then staked the horses and shook out our bedrolls.

"No fire tonight," Calder said.

We stripped off our wet clothes and placed them out to dry, and we used our blankets as robes. I was disappointed that Calder, who had turned his back like a gentleman, did not once try to sneak a look before the blanket was around my shoulders. I did not really know why I was disappointed, because I had expected nothing to happen between us. Calder was not the type of man I had ever been attracted to. He seemed to care little for things like literature and art, and I found his history of vigilantism barbaric.

Our supper was some stale corn bread and wiry beef jerky Calder took from his saddlebag. As we ate, we made the sort of idle conversation expected in such situations.

"Wish we had a can of peaches," Calder said. "And a tin of sardines."

"Wouldn't mind the peaches," I said. "But not with sardines."

"I like oysters, too."

I made a gagging sound.

"Oysters and beer," he said. "Now, that's a meal."

I made a louder gagging sound.

"That's a mess on the floor about an hour after," I said.

"Well, what's your favorite?" he asked. "If you could only eat one meal for the rest of your life, what would it be?"

"This is what men talk about on the trail?" I asked.

"Yeah," Calder said. "Food, beer . . . women."

"In that order?"

"Depends on how long a man has been on the trail," Calder said. "So come now, what's your favorite meal?"

"Brisket," I said. "For dessert, pecan pie."

Then I realized we would soon be facing something quite grave, and I grew weary of the expected.

"Tell me about your wife."

"Why?"

"Because this might be the last chance you have to talk about her."

"This is not a chat I am comfortable having."

"Because I'm a woman?"

"That's part of it."

"Then pretend I'm your boon companion, Orion Wylde. We have come through hell and high winds today and find ourselves hunkered down for the night on a dark plain beneath the Milky Way. Tomorrow we will face mortal danger, yet again. So tell me, as you would your best pal on the trail. What is your best memory of your wife?"

He gave a wistful smile.

"If somebody had asked me that question when she was still alive, I would have imagined that it would have been the marital relations I remembered best," Calder said. "I do, of course, but that's not my favorite memory of Sarah. As the years have passed since she was killed, the memory that comes back to me, again and again, is something that I hardly noticed at the time. It was in the spring, and the boy had not yet turned one, when we were still on the ranch in Presidio County. Satisfied at the end of a long day of work, I was sitting in the shade of a cottonwood tree, with Johnnie on a blanket nearby. Sarah brought me a cup of water. She handed it to me and sat down on the blanket with the boy, touched my knee, and then she smiled—and the whole world seemed right."

He shook his head.

"I've never felt anything was right since," he said. "We were on the trail to Kansas a month later—and found ourselves in the middle of the Red River War."

"What happened?"

"At Sharp's Creek, in the Texas Panhandle, we came upon Quanah Parker and his band of about three hundred Indians," Calder said. "They spotted us, of course. It's hard to hide a wagon loaded with household goods. There was a wagon train in front of us, and they made a run for Adobe Walls, an outpost of buffalo hunters, just north of the Canadian. The train made it. We broke an axle. That was on June seventh."

He rubbed his eyes.

"While Parker assaulted the Walls, a raiding party of Comanche found us and our broken wagon. There were about five of them, on a low ridge maybe three hundred yards away, watching us. We were going to ride away, to leave them the wagon and everything else, because that's what they wanted—they needed food. I had just boosted Sarah up into the saddle of one horse and handed her the boy, then turned to mount the other horse, when I heard Sarah make a pitiful sound. She pitched backward from the saddle before I heard the thunder of the rifle. It was an old fifty-caliber ball. Do you know how big that is? Half an inch in diameter. Bigger around than your thumb."

Calder took a breath.

"The bullet had passed through both her and the boy. They were dead before they hit the ground."

"Oh, God," I said.

"What God?" Calder asked. "There was no God, at least not on Sharp's Creek that day."

"What did you do?"

"Before or after I tracked down and killed three of the war party?" Calder smiled. "That's how I became a bounty hunter. I discovered I have a talent for tracking down and killing people. The three Comanche were dead by nightfall. Then it was dark, and I went back and dug graves for Sarah and the boy, and built a big fire, using parts from the wagon. I kept guard over the bodies to keep the wolves away. Then at dawn I buried them, burned what was left of the wagon and the truck inside, and rode away."

"That's horrific."

"I went to Adobe Walls, where the hunters had driven away Parker with their buffalo rifles, because of their longer range. They packed up and headed home to Dodge City, and I went with them."

"How far are we from—"

"Those graves along Sharp's Creek?" Calder asked. "Sixty or seventy miles, I reckon. You know, it's funny. The Comanche believe that the dead travel the road to the west. I reckon they're right."

He paused.

"I've never told anybody that story," he said. "At least not all of it."

"Do you feel better?"

"No," he said. "There were still two Comanche that got away. Now it's your turn. No holding back. Pretend I'm one of your woman friends and we've just finished low tea or whatever it is that women do before they get down to hen talk. Tell me what you miss most about your lost man."

"That one's easy," I said. "His smell."

31

In the morning, we pulled on our cold and wet clothes and rode along the creek in the direction of *Ciudad Perdida*. The water snaked through a series of rolling hills, and gradually the bluffs got steeper, and soon we were riding right down the middle of the shallow creek.

In an hour, we came upon the broken body of Pollux Adams tangled up in the branches of a willow tree. His neck was bent at an angle that was painful to look at.

"Wonder what it felt like," I mused.

"Which part?" Calder asked. "The flying or the dying?"

"The flying."

"Why don't you ask him?"

"Ghosts can't answer a direct question," I said. "Besides, I don't hear anything. His spirit isn't here. Back at the cabin, maybe."

We urged our horses on.

The banks along the river became steeper, and there began to appear square and rectangular holes here and there—windows and doorways leading to rooms filled with dirt and debris. At the back of my mind, I could hear murmuring voices, but I couldn't make out what they were saying.

"We're getting close," Calder said.

"Do you have a plan?"

"Nope," he said. "I was hoping you'd have one. After all, you're the one who talks to the dead."

I shrugged. "I can hear voices, but they're very old voices," I said. "I don't know what they're saying. They just sound sad, mostly."

We went another quarter of a mile, and the bluff dwellings became thicker along the north side of the creek. In some places, the walls had collapsed, revealing steps going down and rooms that were so big they hadn't been all filled in with dirt yet.

"How many people could have lived here?" I asked.

In my head, the voices had become a chorus of loss.

"Thousands," Calder said. "You've got fresh water here, you're protected from the worst of the winter wind, and there had to be plenty of buffalo and other game. It must not have been a bad life. You could raise a family here."

He was staring at the silver trunk of a cottonwood when he said it, and I knew he was thinking about when he had his own family, not so long ago in Presidio County.

"Come back, Jack."

"I'm here," he said, standing in the saddle and peering down the creek. "There's smoke there, through the trees. I think we are upon the whiskey trader's hideout."

"I see it. And it smells like they're roasting some kind of meat."

"Okay, here's the plan," Calder said decisively. "I am going to ride on in by myself and kill the sonuvabitch, and you're going to wait here. If I don't come back in an hour, you turn that Arabian around and head back toward the trail."

"That's the dumbest plan I ever heard, Jack. First off, we want to bring the whiskey trader back for trial. Second off, if you get in trouble, I'm no good to come in and get you out of it. So it's obvious that I'm the one who has to go in by myself, and you wait here. And if I don't come back soon, then you shoot your way in."

"I don't like it," Calder said. "Maybe we should try to smoke them out first."

"If we were after ordinary criminals, that might work," I said. "But Vanderslice is something there's not even a word for yet, and Malleus isn't even human. I don't think smoke is going to bother them."

"But if you walk in there first, they have you as a hostage."

"I'm only good as a hostage as long as I'm not willing to die," I said. "Jack, you know that I'm not expecting to come out of this alive. Unless I get my aura back, there's no point in my coming out alive. I'll just turn into something more and more ugly. You have to promise that if they threaten to kill me to get you to throw down your guns, that you won't do it. Shoot me if you have to, to prove the point."

"I won't shoot you."

"That's sweet, but not helpful."

Calder smiled.

"Jack," I said. "There's something I need to tell you."

"Well," he said, "me too. But you first."

"There's a thousand-dollar reward out for my capture, dead or alive, in Ohio. I conned a pork baron there out of a few thousand dollars and he squealed pretty loud. So I'm not Kate Bender, but there is a pretty price on my head. If I'm dead when this is over, you ought to ship my body back to Cincinnati and ask for the reward."

He looked a bit odd.

"Now, why the hell would you tell me that?" he asked.

"I'd rather you get the money than County Attorney Sutton," I said. "Now, what is it you want to tell me?"

"It was nothing," he said.

"Nothing?"

"Just that when we get out of this, you should stop cussing in French. It disturbs people. That's all."

Calder dismounted and tied the reins of the horse to a bush. Then he checked his revolver and pulled the rifle from the saddle scabbard and cradled it in one arm. Finally he pulled a cigar from his vest pocket and stuck it in the corner of his mouth.

"All right," he said, "I'm ready. Let's kill us a demon."

I dismounted and handed Fatima's reins over to Calder. Then I closed my eyes, said a silent prayer to whomever or whatever good might listen, and began walking toward the smoke. I was nervous, but I walked deliberately. My head was high, and the breeze trailed the black ribbon behind my hat. They had to hear me coming, because my ankle-high shoes made an awful racket scraping against the gravel and sloshing in the water.

When I rounded a bend in the creek, I saw the hideout, a big complex of ancient rooms tucked into the bluff. The rooms and the stairs going down to them had been cleared of mud, and I could see shadows moving inside.

Outside, on the broad sandbar in front of the complex, stood Vanderslice surrounded by at least a dozen of the wild whackers I had seen before. Some of the whackers were dressed in rags, and others had no clothes at all. They were clustered around a hunk of browned meat being turned on a spit over a fire, and Vanderslice had the bone-handled skinning knife in his hand. He was carving off slices of meat and throwing them to the whackers, who snapped and snarled at one another.

"Down, boys," Vanderslice said. "There's plenty for everyone."

Also on the sandbar was a farm wagon, a buckboard, unhitched but with barrels of whiskey in the back. More barrels were on the sandbar, not far from the stairs leading down into the ancient rooms. Around the barrels were bottles of all shapes and sizes, ready to be filled and corked. An Indian woman and a boy of about twelve were working to fill the bottles, ladling whiskey from the barrels and pouring it into metal funnels in the necks of the bottles, and then stopping the bottles with a cork.

The woman wore a stained buckskin skirt, fringed at the bottom, a blue blouse, and a bead-and-shell necklace around her neck. I could not tell her age. She might have been thirty or fifty. Although her body seemed strong, her face was deeply lined, and her eyes were dark with sorrow. The boy wore dark wool pants, moccasins, and a red print shirt. His bright eyes warily watched Vanderslice as he worked on the meat.

As I drew closer, I could see that what was being turned on the spit was the torso of a man.

"Knew you'd come," Vanderslice said to me, throwing another strip of meat to the whackers. "Women are just dying to meet me."

"I come because of the Russian girl."

His hand went to the pocket with the missing button.

"So . . . what they say about you is true," Vanderslice said. "You do talk to the dead. What did pretty, stupid, dead little Anna have to say?"

"That you betrayed and then killed her."

"But of course," Vanderslice said. "I sold my soul to Malleus."

"I hope it was worth it."

"He'll give me you," he said. "He'll kill you, in the end. But before he does, he'll turn you over to me. And you'll be sorry that you were so rude to me on the street in Dodge City."

"I think not."

"I'm guessing you're not here alone," Vanderslice said, his eyes darting over the creek. "But I reckon we'll find out who and how many soon enough."

"Is that Castor Adams?" I asked.

"The same," he said. "One of the boys did wrong in killing him, but it seemed a shame to let the meat go to waste."

He carved another slice, but instead of throwing it to the whackers, he took a bite. He chewed, then offered it to me.

"Hungry?"

"Not now," I said.

"Oh, it ain't half bad," he said. "I don't see

what all the fuss was, with the Donner Party and old Alfie Packer. Meat is meat. We're all animals, right? Seems to me, a good many human animals would be of more use as vittles anyhow."

He threw the rest of the slice to the whackers. One of them jumped and caught it in his mouth.

"Is Malleus here?"

"In the temple," Vanderslice said, jerking his head back to the ruins.

"Call him out," I said. "I want my soul's shadow back."

Vanderslice laughed. "That ain't going to happen," he said. "Old Malleus is very particular about those shiny bits of stuff that he keeps in a bag on his belt. It's where his power comes from. He reaches up through the solar plexus and snatches them from people. He keeps the bigger and brighter ones, like yours. The others, the dull ones, he uses to turn wolves into whackers."

"So they're not werewolves."

"Just the opposite," Vanderslice said. "Were-men."

"That's why they go back to wolves when you kill them," I said.

"My, you do catch on."

"But what about Shadrach?"

"Oh, he was a real man, all right," Vanderslice answered. "Not much of a man, I'll grant you. Old Malleus had quite enough of his

stupidity after he busted another wheel, so he
shot him with somebody else's aura. When that
happens, it's like two bottles of nitroglycerin
being smashed together—*kaboom!*—it blows
your whole chest apart."

"That's what Malleus uses that antique pistol
on his belt for."

"It's good that you're still dressed for a funeral," Vanderslice said, and smirked. "Because
the next one's going to be your own."

Then something stirred deep in the ruins
Vanderslice called the temple, and I could see
a shadow walking up the stairs. I was expecting
Malleus, but what emerged, instead, into the
daylight was a woman wearing a black silk robe,
open to the waist, with nothing beneath. She
was about my age—and was nearly my image in
every other respect.

Her face was smeared with red ochre, and
abalone baubles dangled from her earlobes.
She moved with an animal grace, like a lazy
housecat walking across a porch warmed by the
sun. The whackers seemed both excited and repelled by her; and even though they scrambled
back out of her way, their hungry eyes locked
on her body.

"Whiskey trader, you talk too much," the
woman said.

"I was only—"

"Shut up," the woman said. Her voice had
the same odd accent that I had detected in
Malleus's voice.

"I should have let Malleus cut out your tongue long ago. How much have you told her? Oh, never mind. I'm going to assume everything."

The woman walked over to me and smiled. She reached out with a cold hand and lifted my chin.

"Now we see through a glass, darkly."

It was Katie Bender.

32

The woman took my left hand in hers and pulled me toward the stone steps leading down into the shadows, but I resisted.

"Come along," she said. "You came here to see Malleus, didn't you?"

"Yes," I said, and stumbled after her. I looked over my shoulder, hoping to catch a glimpse of Calder striding across the gravel bar, but there was nothing but woods and water.

"I've been feeling you for a long while," the woman said. "Years, in fact. Always at the edge of my consciousness, like a half-remembered dream when daylight comes. But here you are in the flesh, at last."

"What should I call you?"

"Ah, there's a problem," she said, stopping. She leaned close and cupped a hand around my ear, brushing away the hair. "Don't call me 'Katie,' because that is a weak and diminutive form of my name. But your modern tongue would break itself in attempting to pronounce 'Aikaterini.'"

"What language is that?"

"Ancient Macedonian."

She kissed me. Her lips were as cold as steel.

"Where are the others?" I asked, pulling away.

"There are no others."

"Ma and Pa Bender? Your brother, John?"

"Ah," she said. "Them. The old ones were merely slaves, and the stupid young one only a consort. They are dead. I killed them all, soon after we left that wretched cabin. As mortals they thirsted after land, and now they have their wish—they sleep beneath the prairie for eternity."

"Did you slit their throats?"

"There was no time for pleasure, darling," she said. "I shot them all, with a marvelous invention—the Colt 1873 revolving pistol, a forty-five-caliber, also called 'the Peacemaker.' Oh, how I love you Americans and your sense of humor!" She laughed wickedly. "Oh, would that Alexander had a thousand such weapons. Macedonians would rule the world still, instead of yet and again."

"You knew Alexander the Great?"

"A casual relationship," she said. "He loved boys more."

"That had to sting."

"Enough talk!" she said. "Malleus awaits."

At the bottom of the steps was a room with a fire pit in the center and all manner of objects piled against the walls: expensive clothes flung carelessly about, caskets overflowing with jewelry, books, marble busts of Greek and Roman statesmen, dusty wine bottles. Also piled about were human skulls the color of parchment. The ghosts here were old—very old. Their voices were the murmur of a shallow river in a deep cave unseen by any man.

Malleus was sitting—or rather squatting—on a throne that looked like it would have been at home in the court of Nero. He was wearing a dressing gown over his enormous body, and from a wide leather belt dangled the antique pistol and the leather bag. His hands were the color of dead fish and were resting on the silver handle of a walking stick.

"Take off your hat," she said.

When I refused, she knocked it to the floor.

Then Katie dropped to one knee and attempted to pull me down with her, but I refused.

"Malleus, my lord," she said. "I have brought the other."

"Welcome to hell," Malleus said, opening his arms. Then he smiled, revealing those teeth the color of old tusk, and I could not help but shudder.

"It could use some cleaning," I said, "but it is hardly my idea of hell."

"Pahghh!" Malleus spat. "You mean your

Christian idea. How bored am I of this theology for simpletons. One god to rule all—how uninspired! Give me that old-time religion, when there was a god for every temper. And hell is merely the netherworld, the place of the dead."

Malleus motioned for Katie to come to him, and she scooted across the floor and put her back against the throne. She loosened the silk gown and he caressed her bare shoulders as he spoke.

"Why have you come here?"

"My aura," I said. "Give it back."

"You had your chance," he said. "I dropped it from surprise when I took it—it was made of better stuff than I expected. It lay there in the mud, and you could have snatched it up, but you did not. I placed it in my collection then. When I have enough of the shiny ones, I will transform into something more pleasing. . . ."

"Are you Macedonian, too?"

He waved dismissively. "I speak more dead languages than any Oxford don," he said. "No man has heard my native tongue in five thousand years, and none know its name. Call it 'Enigma.'"

"Obviously, you aren't human," I said.

"Brilliant," he said. "Any more revelations for us?"

"What are you?"

He smiled. "If I told you," he said, "I might be lying. Or I might not."

I had my answer.

"What are you doing here?"

"Anything I want," he said. "And what I want at the moment—meaning the next hundred years or so—is to set loose a new kind of evil upon humanity. Murder as a kind of sickness. I don't know what to call it yet, exactly. I might just wait and see what kind of bad name you can give it. You get so many things wrong! Oh, some of my favorites—spontaneous generation, the miasma theory of disease, pinochle, maternal imprinting, phrenology, Lamarckism."

"We get a few things right."

"Given enough time, perhaps," he said. "Problem is, your race doesn't have time, does it? What can you accomplish in your biblical three score and ten? The best of you make some music for others to hum, scribble some dreams or nightmares for others to share, or work a lifetime to discover and perfect some new knowledge. But the rest of you—driven by the pursuit of pleasure and profit, turning a blind eye on the pain of others, and always beating ploughshares into swords. Yours is a murderous race. Why, look at what you have done here on the plains in the space of a single generation. You have driven the aborigines from their lands, destroyed a multitude of cultures, and slaughtered the bison to near extinction."

He made a motion with his hand, and Katie

somehow knew what he wanted. She brought him one of the skulls from a pile near the wall.

"Look upon the legacy of an empire," he said, holding up the skull as if he were in a play. "You have no name for them, but they ruled this land for a thousand years and did but a fraction of the harm you have done in a handful. Their empire collapsed, in time. Now, even their name is known only to the wind."

He squeezed the skull, and his fingers crushed the ancient bone as if it were thin plaster; teeth and dust falling to the floor.

"That is man," he said. "That is your fate, and soon. But I offer something . . . better."

"What?" I asked. "You want to turn me into one of those whackers?"

"Why would I do that when I have a surplus of dull auras and an unlimited supply of prairie wolves?" he asked. "No, I want you to serve me as your ageless sister, Aikaterini, serves me. In return, I offer eternal youth, power second only to my own, and a seat at the table of darkness."

"And if I don't?"

"I'll kill you, of course," he said. "Your soul will wither and die without its shadow."

"Doesn't sound like much of a choice."

"Oh, but it is," Malleus hissed. "I can kill you, but I can't make you serve me. You must do that of your own free will. Choose now."

"Thanks, but I'm tired of playing this game,"

I said. "Just give me my aura, and I'll be on my way."

"You're choosing death," he said. "You'll become food for the whackers."

"Well, I always liked dogs."

Where the hell is Calder? I thought.

Malleus struck the cane on the floor, producing a rap that echoed from the walls.

"Enough!" he said. "There is one last thing you should see."

He nodded to Katie, and she stood, picked up a clay jar by the throne, and removed the wooden plug. She shook some handfuls of blue powder into her hand and threw them into the fire pit.

The fire erupted like she had thrown kerosene on it.

It continued to blaze fiercely, with a weird blue tinge, and Malleus began chanting in the Enigma language. Presently a form appeared in the flames. It was a nude man, a young man with blond hair.

It was Jonathan.

Suddenly I couldn't breathe. I felt like the floor would sink from beneath me. I staggered back a step or two.

"This is a trick," I muttered. "Something you've ordered from Sylvestre and Company. It's not real."

The nude Jonathan stepped out of the fire and into the room. Katie padded over and looped an arm around his neck and nuzzled his cheek.

"Oh, he seems real enough to me," she said hungrily.

"Get away from him!"

I shoved her aside.

"Jonathan," I said. "Is it you?"

He smiled, just as I remembered. He was still the age he was when he died. And when once I had been so much younger than he, now I was *older*. Nearly twice as old. Would he still want me now?

"Jonathan, are you real?"

No response. He seemed confused.

"Ask him," Malleus said. "Ask him for the secret sign, the message that you had agreed that he would send from the other side as a sign that love survives death."

I took his hand and squeezed it against my cheek.

"Do you remember?"

He blinked.

"Do you remember me?"

"Ophelia," he said.

"My love," I said. "What was the message?"

"J'attends ma femme."

It was the message: "I await my wife."

I sank to the floor beside him, sobbing, still holding his precious hand against my cheek.

"Oh God," I said.

Katie put a hand on his shoulder and urged him down with me. I cupped his face in my hands and kissed him, a kiss that thrilled me to my shadowless soul. Then I rested my head against his chest.

And frowned.

"This isn't right," I said.

"What could not be right?" Katie asked. "It is your love, returned from the grave. This is your heart's desire. All of your prayers have been answered in an instant, and you can stay here and rule with us—and live with him—forever."

I got to my feet. My head was spinning, and I had to think hard to get out the words.

"This is a trick," I said. "It's not Jonathan."

"But the message," Malleus said. "What of the message?"

"I—I don't know," I said. "You read my mind, somehow. Maybe you even read my heart. But it's not him. I know it's not him. It can't be."

"Why not?"

"He doesn't *smell* right."

At that, the Jonathan-like apparition vanished in a flash of light and thunder and blue smoke. I fell backward from the concussion, landing heavily on the stone floor, my head throbbing.

Malleus stepped down from the throne and walked around the fire pit to where I lay on the floor. He looked down at me like I was a pile of trash, something annoying that needed to be cleaned up.

"Tell the whiskey peddler to feed her to the whackers," Malleus said.

"Shame," Katie said, walking over to me on swiveling hips. "We would have found her amusing . . . for a time."

Then she reached down and grabbed hold of my earlobe and pulled me to my feet. I knocked her hand away with a forearm.

"That hurts, you bitch."

She laughed.

"You dare defy me?" she asked. "Your suffering will be great."

I reached up and grabbed one of the alabaster earrings.

"You first."

I jerked the thing out of her ear and threw it to the ground. She shrieked and clasped her hand to her ear. Blood ran down the side of her neck. Then she looked at me with a hatred that made my heart skip a beat.

I made a dash for the steps.

She scrambled after me, and I was nearly at the top when she caught my ankle and pulled me down. I fell, but kicked out hard with my free leg. The heel of my shoe landed squarely in Katie Bender's face, and she fell backward down the stairs.

I emerged from the steps into the sunshine.

"Stop her!" Katie Bender called.

Vanderslice was standing with his arms crossed, the bone-handled skinning knife in his right hand, and he was smiling. He was about ten yards away, between me and the creek.

Katie Bender made it to the top of the steps.

Blood was gushing from her nose and the corner of her mouth. She wiped her mouth with the palm of her hand, smearing the blood across her cheek.

"Didn't know immortals bled," I said.

"You fool," she said. "This isn't *my* blood. I'll just replace it with my next victim. And I'm going to start with you. Toss me the knife, whiskey trader."

Vanderslice tossed the skinning knife over my head, a perfect pitch, and Katie Bender caught the bone handle in her left hand. Then she approached, the knife at the ready.

I stumbled backward, into Vanderslice.

He pinned my arms to my side.

"I'm going to slit your throat from ear to ear," she said.

"Get back!"

"Then I'm going to skin you and throw your hide in with the others, and you're going to end up becoming a belt for some kind of machine back East, turning out spools for thread or toothpicks or maybe hammer handles."

"Don't touch me!"

"Are you going to beg?" she asked. "There would be some pleasure in that."

Vanderslice grabbed my hair and jerked my head back, exposing my throat.

Katie Bender placed the point of the knife beneath my right ear.

"Beg," she taunted. "I want to hear you beg

until your words are just bloody bubbles oozing from your neck."

"*Bon Dieu* and all my ancestors," I mumbled, recalling the first prayer that Tanté Marie had taught me. "Give me breath to vanquish those who torment me."

Then I blew in her face.

There was the crack of a rifle from across the creek and something hit Katie Bender like a hammer. She was knocked off her feet and the bone-handled knife spun from her fingers and skittered on the gravel.

She sat up slowly.

Her black silk robe was parted, revealing an ugly hole between her breasts, with blood and gore spilling from it.

"This can be fixed," she said weakly.

Then the whackers, smelling the blood, began clustering around. They were on all fours, sniffing and snarling.

"Malleus!" she called. "There is little time."

Then the first whacker lunged, and I could not tell if it was in the form of a man or a wolf, but I could see bright teeth tearing at her throat. Then the others were on her, and one of them that was still a man snatched up the bone-handled knife and began slashing with it.

Katie Bender's screams died amid a geyser of blood.

I looked away.

33

Vanderslice released my arms and backed away from the horror.

"Stop right there!" Calder shouted.

Calder was wading from the creek onto the gravel bar. The big rifle was held at waist level in both of his hands. The unlit cigar was still jammed in the corner of his mouth.

Vanderslice pulled his six-shooter and turned.

"Drop the iron," Calder said. "You're under arrest for murder."

"Jack Calder," the whiskey trader sneered. "Always the vigilante, aren't you?"

"I aim to take you back to stand trial," Calder said. "But I'd settle for putting a five-hundred-grain bullet down your throat. What'll it be?"

Vanderslice let the pistol fall.

"Get down," Calder ordered, pulling his own big revolver while placing the rifle on the gravel. "On your knees. Turn around. Do it, damn you."

Vanderslice fell to his knees, and Calder

kicked him between the shoulders, sending him stomach-first on the gravel. He aimed the revolver at the back of Vanderslice's head.

"Maybe I ought to settle things here," Calder said. "Save the Ford County taxpayers the cost of a trial. How do you feel about a slug in the back of your head? That's a lot kinder than what you did to that poor Russian girl."

Vanderslice's eyes were wide with fear.

"No, Jack!" I shouted.

"Why not? He would have killed you. You know what he is."

"I know," I said. "The question is, what are we?"

"Damn it," Calder said, and pulled a pair of iron handcuffs from his pocket.

"Put these on him," he said, tossing me the cuffs. "Just clamp them to his wrists and make sure they lock. Make 'em real tight."

In a moment, I had the whiskey trader's hands locked behind his back.

The frenzied whackers were still working on Katie Bender.

"What the hell is that?" Calder asked me.

"You got the hell part right," I said.

"Are they men or something else?"

"Something else," I said. "These, you should kill."

Calder raised the revolver and emptied it into the pack, sending dead wolves flying. The rest backed away, snarling, while Calder reloaded his revolver from cartridges in his shirt pocket. There wasn't much left on the ground of Katie Bender—parts of one hand and a foot, some chunks of meat and splintered bones.

Crows called raucously from a tree on top of the bluff.

Calder again emptied the revolver at the pack. Again he reloaded. Two of his rounds had missed their mark and pierced the barrels behind. Whiskey ran on the ground toward the steps.

A whacker came around and tried to get at us from the creek side, but Calder turned and put a bullet in the wild man's chest. He fell back, and by the time he reached the water, he was a dead wolf.

"Where's the demon?" Calder asked.

"Here," Malleus said. He was standing at the top of the steps, the ancient pistol upraised in his right hand. "Your next question is whether this *amateur* has recovered her aura. I'm sorry to disappoint, but it is still safe in my collection."

"Hand it over," Calder said.

His pistol was leveled at Malleus.

"No."

Calder fired.

Malleus shrugged.

Calder fired twice more. The bullets passed through the creature and pierced the barrels behind him. More whiskey gurgled to the ground.

"This is a forty-four-caliber Russian," Calder said. "It should have killed him."

"Told you," I said.

"Guns have no effect on me," Malleus said. "But I can certainly make use of them. Observe."

He whistled and called the last of the whackers. The wild man slunk over, low to the ground, his head down in submission. Malleus urged him to stand. When he did, the demon fired the pistol at him.

The whacker's chest exploded with a flash that looked like lightning and sounded like thunder.

Pieces of dead wolf littered the gravel.

Smoke curled from the barrel of the antique pistol. The crows were flitting overhead, made bold by the smell of carrion.

"Impressive, isn't it?" Malleus asked, sloshing powder from a flask into the muzzle of the pistol. Then he reached into his bag and came out with a fistful of auras.

"Let's see which of the bright ones we have here," he said.

He opened his palm, revealing six auras of varying sizes and colors. They glittered like jewels in his palm. The largest was violet and yellow and blue, swirling in harmony.

"That's mine," I cried.

"Give it to her," Calder said.

"This one?" he asked. He tossed the other auras on the gravel and held mine between his pale thumb and forefinger, lifting his hand to the sun. "It is my favorite. Oh, look how it shines!"

Then a black bird wheeled and dove and plucked the aura from his fingers.

"Pahghh!" Malleus cried. "The raven!"

It was Eddie.

Malleus raised the pistol and fired impotently. He had not yet loaded an aura into it. He dropped the gun and ran, with surprising speed, to where the woman and child were cowering near the wagon.

He snatched the child from the woman's arms and made a waddling run for the steps.

"Come after me," he said, "and I'll kill the child—then I'll eat his soul."

The woman dropped to her knees and began to wail.

Then Malleus ran down the steps.

Calder reloaded. Then he picked up Vanderslice's pistol and put it in his belt.

"Jack, what are you doing?"

"Going after him."

"But the boy," I said.

"What about the little bastard?" Calder asked. "*Comanchitos* grow up to be warriors, and warriors kill innocent women and children. Best to stop them now, before they get the chance."

"He's just a boy."

The mother was crying even louder, on her knees, begging for her son.

"We should kill the mother, too. She could produce more young."

"Jack, they didn't kill Sarah and Johnnie.

They didn't kill your family. You're blinded by hate. It's Malleus, Jack. He's making you act this way. He feeds off misery, and he's using your grief against you."

"They should die," he said.

"Remember how you love justice, Jack?" I asked. "Do you remember how the whiskey trader put the body of the dead girl on the meridian marker to show his contempt for justice? His contempt for *you*?"

Calder rubbed his eyes. "These aren't the Indians that killed Sarah and Johnnie?"

"No, Jack. Fight the hate."

"All right," he said. "I'm all right now."

"You're sure?"

He nodded. "What now?" Calder asked. "How do you kill a demon?"

"Don't know," I said. "But I'd better figure it out soon, because I'm going back down there. Lead doesn't work, so we have to try something else—after we get the boy out."

"You can't."

"I must," I said.

"Okay, then," he said. "Let's go."

We walked down the steps, following the trail of whiskey that had leaked from the barrels. It had pooled at the bottom, and rivulets were spreading across the stone floor.

Malleus was on his throne, the frightened boy on his lap.

I stopped twenty feet away, on the near side

of the fire pit, and placed a hand on Calder's forearm.

"No closer," I said. "Don't get near the demon's hands."

"Enough!" Malleus said. "I am nothing if not a businessman, and it is time to strike a bargain. I'll let the boy go in exchange for you, Ophelia Wylde."

"Not on your life," Calder said.

A finger of whiskey inched across the floor toward the throne. Malleus made an ugly sound and moved away, dragging the boy with him. His yellow eyes kept glancing down at the whiskey.

"Bothered by something?" I asked.

"You for the boy," Malleus said. "Quick, quick!"

He was sidling around toward us.

I stepped across one of the rivulets of whiskey and pulled Calder across with me. Malleus stopped.

"What are you afraid of?" I asked.

"Trade!" he said, and squeezed the boy until he cried out in pain.

I knelt down, dipped my fingers in the growing puddle, and smelled it.

"Whoa," I said. "It's not like the bourbon my father drank, but it must be at least eighty proof. Is that what you're afraid of, the alcohol?"

Malleus said nothing.

"Give us the boy," I said.

I stepped forward, following the streams of whiskey.

Malleus backed away.

There was a puddle of whiskey in the depression near the fire pit, and I knelt and cupped some in my right hand. Then I stood and flung the stuff at Malleus. He cried out, his hands going up to protect his face. Drops of whiskey sizzled and burned where they landed on his skin.

"Run!" I cried, but the boy was already in motion.

Malleus ran after him, but the boy jumped over a wet patch in the floor and landed in Calder's arms. Malleus stopped on the other side of the whiskey like he'd hit a stone wall.

I flung more whiskey at Malleus while Calder ran up the steps with the boy. Then I got a double handful from the puddle and flung it at him.

Then I ran as well.

"No," Malleus called. "Mercy! I will grant you anything. . . ."

At the top, the boy was already in his mother's arms. Calder was rolling a barrel over, and as soon as I was clear, he kicked it down the steps. We could hear it bound and skip down and then crash open on the floor. Then the flood of whiskey must have hit the fire pit, because there was a *whoosh* followed by a great blue flash and waves of heat.

"More," I said.

We both wrestled barrels over and let them roll down the steps.

"Please," Malleus cried. "The world is yours for the asking!"

Now the Indian woman and the boy were helping to roll barrels over and letting them tumble down the steps, adding to the conflagration. Flames belched up from the steps and twisted toward the sky.

Malleus began to beg in Enigma.

"What language is that?" Calder asked.

"Nobody alive knows," I said.

Now Malleus was screaming in Enigma.

Three more barrels and we had used up all the whiskey, except for the full bottles, which the woman and the child were tossing into the flames. Then there was a furious popping, like firecrackers going off, and there shot from the flames rays of glittering color: red and brown and green and blue. The colors rocketed over our heads and shot into the sky.

"Was that him?" Calder asked.

"The auras," I said. "They'll find their owners . . . eventually."

"What about the ones he dropped?"

We found the five others on the gravel and threw them down the steps into the blaze. We watched as they shot over our heads in streaks of red and orange and yellow.

Then the earth trembled and Calder pulled me back. There was a great cracking sound and the bluff face collapsed, sealing inside whatever was left of Malleus.

The dust from the collapse rolled toward us, like a fog.

I stood a moment, shaking.

Then Eddie flapped down, wheeled around us once, and landed on the seat of the wagon. He still had my aura in his beak. I walked over to him and he jumped up on my shoulder. I held out my right hand and he dropped the aura in my palm.

I stared at the swirling colors.

"That's you?" Calder asked.

"That's me," I said.

Then the aura began to shine even more brilliantly—and melted into my palm. It coursed down my arm and into my chest, where it made a tight, warm glow beneath my heart.

34

Calder dug a grave and buried what was left of Castor Adams, but he left the remains of Katie Bender for the crows. We found my Arabian and Calder's bay and hitched them to the wagon. We put Vanderslice in the back of the buckboard, his hands still cuffed, and asked his Comanche wife and child if they wanted to return with us to Dodge City. The woman shook her head, took the child by the hand, and began walking down the creek to the west.

"Where are they going?" I asked.

"I don't know," Calder said. "But anywhere has to be better than here."

Three days later, we crossed the wooden toll bridge over the Arkansas River and drove up Bridge Street. Calder pulled the buckboard to a stop in front of the city offices, where Tom the Jailer was sitting outside, his chair tipped back and his red-flecked boots propped on a rain barrel. He was drinking coffee from an enameled tin cup.

"What do you have there?" Tom called.

"The murderer Vanderslice," Calder said. "We arrested him on a federal warrant for peddling whiskey in the territory, but I expect that Judge Grout will want him held for the murder of the girl found on the meridian marker."

"Thunder," Tom said, pitching the coffee and rising from the chair. "You must have caught him not far out of town. Give him to me. I've got just the place for him."

Vanderslice had gone insane in the middle of No Man's Land. He was babbling about demons and wolves as Tom helped him down from the rear of the wagon. Then he began to describe how the weremen had eaten up Katie Bender after Calder shot her.

"What's he talking about?" Tom asked.

"Damned if I know," Calder said.

"What day is today?" I asked.

"Monday," Tom said.

"We've been gone a whole week," I said.

"What do you mean?" Tom asked. "You were here yesterday morning, when Doc McCarty ordered the Russian girl dug up from Boot Hill. I loaned you some clothes, remember?"

Calder and I exchanged puzzled looks.

"It's the twenty-first, right?" Calder asked.

"You're a week off." Tom laughed. "Today's the fourteenth."

Calder turned to me.

"But how is that possible?" he asked.

"You two are sure acting strange," Tom said. "Are you sure you didn't catch some crazy from the whiskey trader?"

"It seems like a whole week has passed," I said. "That's what Jack means."

"All righty," Tom said, shaking his head.

"What time is it?" I asked.

"Well, the westbound train has just pulled into the depot," Tom said. "That means it must be a quarter to nine, give or take."

"The hearing," Calder said. "Let's hope the train is early."

"Where can I find a dress?" I asked.

I bought a dress—a white dress—at Rath's mercantile, and ducked in the back of the store to pull it on. When I emerged, and Calder expressed his approval, I told him not to get used to it. While I rushed to the courthouse, Calder went to find Doc McCarty and tell him about the capture of Vanderslice.

In the courtroom, I found Potete already at the defense table. On the other side, Sutton was talking in low tones with a white-haired gentleman.

Judge Grout was on the bench, with his pocket watch out.

"I'm glad you could join us, Miss Wylde," Grout said, snapping the watch shut. "It is now eight fifty-nine. You had exactly one minute to spare."

"I apologize, Your Honor."

I took my seat next to Potete.

Calder took a bench in the back.

Then Grout told Sutton to get on with it.

"A moment, Your Honor," Sutton said, and turned back to the white-haired man. The man was looking over at me, and he and Sutton exchanged some furious whispers.

"I told you to get on with it," Grout said. "I won't ask again."

Sutton nodded and then made a show of straightening the papers on his side of the desk. Next he cleared his throat and announced that the state was dropping the charges.

"What?" Grout asked.

"The state is dropping the complaint," Sutton said, then coughed. "We move for dismissal."

"Why?" Grout demanded.

"Insufficient evidence," Sutton said.

"All right, drop the lawyering," Grout said, shaking the handle of the gavel at Sutton. "Just tell me straight what is going on here. Who's that gentleman with you?"

"Your Honor, I'm Colonel Alexander York," the man said, standing, and he suddenly seemed imposing. Even though he had white hair, he wasn't that old—forty or forty-five, perhaps. "I'm a member of the Grand Army of the Republic and a former state senator from Independence. I was summoned here by an urgent telegram from the county attorney to identify the fugitive murderess, Katie Bender."

Sutton was looking down at the desk.

"You are in a position to do so?" Grout asked.

"I met the woman in 1874 while searching for my late brother, Dr. William York, who disappeared on the Osage Trail—may he rest in peace."

"Go on."

"This woman is *not* Kate Bender."

Grout crossed his arms.

"But you have to admit," Sutton said, "that she bears a striking resemblance."

"I'll admit to nothing of the sort," Colonel York said. "I would recognize the murderess who killed my brother—her image is burned into my brain. If this woman is Kate Bender . . . why, I'm the queen of England!"

"What do you have to say for yourself, Counselor?" Grout asked.

"I apologize," Sutton said. "It was an honest mistake."

"You'll do more than apologize to Colonel York and Miss Wylde," Grout said. "You'll make sure that all their expenses are covered, and from your own pocket. I don't want this fiasco to cost the citizens of Ford County one thin dime. Is that understood?"

"Yes, Your Honor."

"This case is dismissed—with extreme prejudice."

Grout banged his gavel so hard I thought it would break.

"So that's it," I said. "I'm free."

Potete leaned over to whisper in my ear. "There is just one more thing," he said.

I told him I couldn't imagine what it would be.

"Armbruster," he said. "He's waiting for you."

35

Potete led me to a room across the hall from the courtroom that was normally used for attorneys to consult with their clients. The door was closed, and he paused before opening it.

"I'm sorry," he said. He seemed strangely sober.

"Oh, I was expecting this day," I said. "Not so soon, perhaps, but eventually. How'd he find me?"

"I wired Chicago to ask about this Sylvestre fellow you had mentioned, hoping that it might prove useful," Potete said. "But Potter Palmer's spies must be everywhere, because Armbruster came nearly at once. So it is all my fault."

"Don't be so hard on yourself," I said. "This is my fault. It's my mess. I'll face the music."

Potete nodded.

He opened the door, and I stepped inside.

Armbruster was standing at the window, looking out, his hands clasped behind his back.

The sun was so bright outside that he was just a silhouette framed in the glass.

"Close the door," he said.

I gently shut the door behind me.

There was no furniture in the room except a wooden desk and two uncomfortable-looking chairs. On the desk was an inkwell and pen.

"Have a seat, Mrs. Wylde."

I sat down on my side of the table.

"Do you know why I'm here?" he asked.

"Potter Palmer sent you."

"That's right," he said.

"You're Mr. Palmer's . . . troubleshooter."

"That's right," he said. "I fix problems for him. And I'm here to fix a problem called 'Ophelia Wylde.'"

Then he turned, pushed his hat back to the crown of his head, and I saw his face. He was balding, and his skin was so white, it didn't look like he'd ever spent a day in the sun. His eyes stared at me through a pair of pince-nez glasses, which perched on the bridge of his nose.

"How much will it take to fix this problem?"

"I beg your pardon?"

"How much?" he asked, placing his hands on the table and leaning forward. "Don't be coy. You must have a figure in mind. What Mr. Palmer wishes is for no embarrassment to come to him or to Mrs. Palmer. For that, he is prepared to buy your silence. If you agree never to speak of your association with Potter Palmer, we are prepared to pay you one thousand dollars."

I laughed. I couldn't help myself.

"Very well," he said. "Three thousand."

"Oh, my." I was struggling to catch my breath. "This is too much."

"Five thousand," Armbruster said, fuming. "But that is the absolute limit. And you must sign the agreement now."

He removed a legal-looking paper from his coat pocket, unfolded it, and placed it on the table. He showed me where to sign, and I was still giggling as I took the pen, dipped it in ink, and scribbled my name at the bottom.

"Very good," he said, whisking the document away, folding it, and tucking it into the inside pocket of his suit. Then he removed a fat envelope from another pocket and counted out five thousand dollars in National Gold Bank Notes.

Then he tipped his hat and left, leaving the door open behind him.

I picked up the bills, then realized I had no pockets.

Calder appeared in the doorway.

"What was that all about?"

"I can't really tell you," I said, shoving the bills in his hands. "Here, put this in your pocket before I lose it."

"What in the world?"

"Don't let me spend it," I said. "Most of it is going to pay a debt in Cincinnati. What's left over—well, that I can spend. Just for the essentials, for me and Eddie."

"If you say so."

"I do."

He shoved the money in his pocket.

"There's another train this afternoon," he said. "Going west."

"What are you talking about?"

"You'll be wanting to leave now, I reckon," he said. "Maybe you'll want to stay for the service in the morning on Gospel Ridge. The Russian girl's family has come to claim her body, but it didn't seem right to send her off without a service. So Doc McCarty organized it. He said they don't speak much English, but they worked it out."

"That's nice," I said. "I'll stay for that."

Calder nodded.

"You know, we made a pretty good team."

"We did," Calder said.

"There could be some advantage to our teaming up."

"What do you mean?"

"Partners," I said. "A bounty hunter and a medium who talks to the dead. Murder, a specialty. Special rates for demons and ancient evils."

"Detectives," he said.

"Why not?" I asked. "I can see the sign now, maybe over an office near Doc McCarty's place on North Front. Calder and Wylde, Consulting Detectives—what do you think?"

"We could try it," he allowed. "On a month-to-month basis."

"Of course," I said. "Because I'm still headed west. Eventually. Then it's settled."

We shook hands.

Calder allowed himself a smile.

"Breakfast?" he asked.

"Absolutely," I said. "But I have to get out of these awful clothes first."